What Could a Priest Know

about Marriage?

Rev. Martin L. Dunne III

WALDORF PUBLISHING

Published by Waldorf Publishing
2140 Hall Johnson Road
#102-345
Grapevine, Texas 76051
www.WaldorfPublishing.com

What Could a Priest Know about Marriage?: How to
prepare for, find, and keep that one special relationship

ISBN: 978-1-64921-484-3

Library of Congress Control Number: 2020940372

Copyright © 2020

Design by Baris Celik

This book is dedicated to the one who gently, perfectly showed me what love is.

Table of Contents

Introduction

"Happy the one who finds wisdom, the one who gains understanding! Her profit is better than profit in silver, and better than gold is her revenue; She is more precious than corals, and no treasure of yours can compare with her."

— Proverbs 3:13-15

Many priests have lamented to me about their concern over the frequency they have been asked this question: "How can a priest, someone who is not even married, have a clue about marriage?"

You could say the same thing about Jesus, about whom all records indicate a perpetually unmarried status. Over two billion Christians believe Jesus is God. So, how could God *not* know about marriage? I believe much of my Judeo-Christian background can reinforce the notion that God is not only the quintessential expert on marriage, but that he also created the institution of marriage. We were all created for a purpose; most of us were created for marriage as part of our purpose, but we were all created with longing for communion. The *very first* instruction given by God to Adam and Eve was to create a family: *"God blessed them and God said to them: Be fertile and multiply."* (Gen 1:28).

Through much of my life I have had the same particular thought regarding marriage; the same particular thought that many have echoed to me throughout life: fulfillment and happiness are found in many ways, but in a unique way through romantic love and marriage. I believe we all are created with something needed in order to arrive at fulfillment regardless of vocation: our ability to love the same way we have already been loved. I recognize life has its pains which seem to defy explanation, but my belief is that each of us was created by God for a unique mission to love in a way no one else in time was meant to live, all out of his love for us. Each of us received various unique combinations of blessings, all out of his love for us, whether directly or indirectly. The ability to at least strive to love the way we have already been loved by God is the key to remaining committed to the life you were created to live. It is the must which contributes to our ultimate happiness, whether that looks like marriage, that looks like priesthood, or that looks like something else altogether different.

Although founded on both scholastic teachings and experience, much of what I have said to others has been easily dismissed. *What Could a Priest Know about Marriage?* contains challenges throughout, but I assure you that it will be worth your time and efforts. I admit my content may be intimidating. Nevertheless, with what is said in this book and elsewhere, I hope you reject the excuses not to go about things the right way. It can be extremely easy for all of us to find many excuses not to do what we are meant to do. Making excuses not to act is one of the most harmful things we can do towards both ourselves and others. Yes, most recognize that life is full of unavoidable challenges and pain, and we can have the tendency to avoid unnecessary pain. Connected with that is the frequent conclusion that avoiding pain involves staying in our perceived comfort zones. We have a tendency to remain where we feel there will be the least amount of danger of harm from any fears which seem to threaten that trace of perceived comfort. There can be fear that more may be asked of us than we can handle. There can be fear of the rejection we may have to face. There can be fear that all our efforts will be for nothing, so it's more comfortable not to bother.

Pope Emeritus Benedict XVI concluded, "You were not made for comfort, you were made for greatness." Excuses may provide us with that feeling of relief which makes us conclude that the pressure is gone, but the reality is we are often depriving ourselves of our greatest opportunities to live, love and fulfill our purpose. By avoiding the possibility of the passing pain which may have been demanded with our efforts, we may be depriving ourselves of a lasting happiness that would have definitely been worth the cost many times over.

There are opportunities we may never have again; as time is always moving forward and circumstances are always changing in virtually infinite combinations. A phrase which has at once caused me both consolation and trepidation is, "Once a moment passes the seal of eternity is on it, eternally unchangeable." This statement is so very true. The most qualified scientists seem to unanimously acknowledge the impossibility of travelling backwards in time. Once a moment passes, it is unalterable. We either created a happy memory or a moment of regret. Either way it is an event which can never be changed or undone.

The excuses for not doing what we are meant to do may seem logical in the moment, but they are illogical for, at the very least, our long term well-being. For example, I think it is illogical to think that we will fail in every opportunity to improve. Even if we seem to fail, we still gain invaluable insights that prepare us for new opportunities. We need to always strive to do everything we can to arrive at the ultimate purpose of our existence. Most people also seem to forget the added bonus that while we are striving towards our ultimate purpose in each moment, we can rest in the likelihood we are also living our purpose within each particular moment. Although I cringe when I think of all the times I forgot this, of all the times I allowed my created excuses to hold me back, those scenarios continue, even three decades later in some cases, to serve as the best motivations to insure I do not repeat my mistakes as much as possible!

I feel all of my knowledge is gained in a parallel way to how Walt Disney garnered all of his own achievements: "Sometimes I think of myself as a little bee. I go from one area of the studio to another and gather pollen and sort of stimulate everybody." In other words, he used what he learned from observations from his own life, and often the lives of others, to help everyone become their very best.

The insights in this book have true value because they are incorporation of so many observations and experiences of life, starting with those who did not hold back in sharing with me their insights on the best way to approach relationships. This started with the outstanding, heroic, selfless, and sacrificial example of my own parents. Their actions demonstrated more than words often could, selflessly making many sacrifices for each other and for the sake of their four children. After nearly five decades of marriage I feel they are closer and more in love with each other than ever before. Along with my parents dozens of other couples from several generations have candidly offered their secrets to their "success."

I certainly strove to incorporate what I learned as I went through my own first hand experiences: Twelve separate times I sought that lifelong relationship through women of various backgrounds. Twice those relationships developed into the level of having long-term girlfriends, and once I was engaged. From these experiences over a large part of my life I feel I can write a dedicated book simply on, "what *not* to do in dating." While I believe almost everyone has insights to share in this department, I will offer some of my most painful, yet profound, lessons in my hopes of at least sparing others the unnecessary pain I went through and inadvertently caused.

I also recognize how the dynamics from every other area of life and every other type of relationship outside of dating can influence how the romantic relationships progress. Yes there was much value gleaned from my schoolyears, but I particularly see the value gained from the chapter of life which occurred in the eight years between my college graduation and my return to college through the seminary. During the eight years I earned my CPA, worked in the world in entry-level, supervisory, and managerial roles, owned and took care of my own home, volunteered in churches and ministries at the local, state, and international levels for various worthwhile endeavors, and led two non-profit organizations.

Learning about relationships certainly continued after entering seminary. After all, seminary means seedbed, the institution where individuals discern, develop and prepare for the priesthood over several years of intense academic, spiritual, and pastoral pursuits in a variety of challenging settings around the world. During this time I completed several undergraduate-level and graduate-level courses on marriage, relationships, and counseling and ministry from four accredited universities in two states. I also participated in dozens of practicums in a variety of ministerial settings found in various settings of life, including churches, retreats, hospitals, nursing homes, and schools.

More than ever I realize the learning will never end. If anything, the rate of learning has accelerated since becoming a priest. I feel the prime motivator has been the growing awareness of the intensity, sensitivity, and dynamics of most relationships. The majority of my years of formal ministry, as a complement to the experiences from various service projects throughout life, have been with those in the various stages of romantic love: from those in their preparations for marriage, to those in the early stages of adjusting together to the various unexpected bumps which threaten marriages, to those who were married for several decades and were more truly in love than ever before through their conviction that they are truly soulmates. These encounters with each couple empowered me through gaining more insights and more connections which allowed me to offer more help, and more hope, to other couples. At the very least the insights I offered contributed to their awareness of breakthrough realizations of which they were previously unaware.

So, "What is love?" Most have ideas of what it is certainly *not*! Yet, I am afraid most, including myself for much of my life, still could not answer that question very well at all. I do not claim to know everything. I do, however, have my convictions. It has occurred at least dozens of times already, but every time I held a conviction about something or someone it was proven true. My eyes are just now beginning to open, and if nothing else I realize they will keep opening forever. I believe God placed, within the very core of us, the longing to receive love. However, I also believe that the deeper longing, given by God, is to *give* love. Nothing seems more countercultural today than this form of true love. Many in our society go no further than asking "What's in it for me?" This hedonistic attitude seems to be an obsession we are reminded of in so many ways. Ironically this is the biggest obstacle towards finding self-contentment. This is because I realize that the truer the gesture of love, the more the giver naturally benefits. More often than not, the greatest gestures of loving seem to frequently occur when it is the last thing one feels like doing, whether because of mood, lack of energy, lack of time, other preferences, or all of these factors combined. I hope this book will open your eyes to the awareness that although most of the aspects of true love are those often sadly dismissed by many as unpleasant and avoidable, they are actually traits for the most direct paths towards true freedom and happiness.

While a lot of what I write about may come across as a fairy tale, true love is actually the greatest reality which we are all called to partake of in one way or another. While I would never for a moment want to preach, I feel I cannot talk about love without talking about God. Sadly I feel God has had a worse rap than maybe ever before. In some instances He is presented as a consolation prize for losers that have nothing else. Or even worse, God is depicted as an ogre instead of the one who can love us better than anyone else could.

I believe that all eternity will be necessary in order to understand who God truly is. The first letter of John declares that God *is* love, and because of that reality love has to be absolute. True love is holding absolutely nothing back. The one who created everything showed us His love by holding absolutely nothing back. He let go of everything in love, but He also let go of everything in trust that it would be worth it. Many accept that this love was demonstrated from Jesus' cross. All of us are called to express that same love, and in a particularly special way. Every personal relationship is meant to express that love, and that is especially evident in marriage. But, people rarely seem to realize this love because in one way or another, something is held back. For example, one reason for annulment, a formal process where the Church concludes that the requirements necessary to have a marriage were missing, is the signing of a prenuptial agreement without a very good reason. I continue to pray that more people recognize that part of their path to happiness involves letting go, as much as possible, in a spirit of true love and trust.

Again, no one understood this better than Jesus, who said *"everyone who has given up houses or brothers or sisters or father or mother or children or lands for the sake of my name will receive a hundred times more"* (Mat. 19:29). Although I believe not everyone is expected to give up these particular blessings in the same way a religious brother may be asked, I can certainly attest to the meaning of this verse from my firsthand experience. Saying yes to the seminary cost me my career, my home, virtually everything inside it, my savings, and several of my relationships. While I still do not own real estate or furniture, I have a fulfillment that, in my opinion, was worth the cost of a million times over!

A far more profound example from recent history is Mother Teresa. As a teenager she left everything she had ever known in Europe to serve in the most impoverished part of India. From what little she had, what little she was able to give, she would go on to successfully establish missions which continue to directly assist millions in their basic needs in every remote corner of the world. In spite of this, perhaps her most famous quote is, "It does not matter if we are successful as much as if we are faithful."

This quote may seem out of place in this book. In one form or another we all long for success. Many will read this book in hopes of finding that one true relationship. They may strive to carefully incorporate every idea which springs from this text. And yet nothing may *seem* to change. Nothing may *seem* to improve. Please believe that for your efforts things are always progressing, that things are developing, and that things are growing towards that ultimate fulfillment for which you long. For example, you may give an admirable, total effort towards trying to make a relationship work. But, no matter what you do or do not do, love cannot be forced. Thank God! You should never want anything less than to have someone who is meant to love you as much as you are meant to love them. Even if a relationship does not work out, please believe you never wasted your time and energy. If nothing else, you have gained new wisdom from your experiences on how to be better going forward. If you have not found fulfillment yet, please always keep your eyes open. One of the happiest lessons I have ever learned, and have been reminded of frequently in every stage of life, is that the best things seem to happen when they are least expected.

There is also the possibility that you will never meet that special particular individual who you were meant to marry. It sounds harsh; it sounds unfair. There are many potential reasons for this. We live in a fallen world where there is so much evil and selfishness that innocent people suffer the consequences. Maybe the person you were meant to marry was prevented from even meeting you through no fault of their own. One of my best childhood friends lost his life as a young teenager because another friend thought he was playing with an empty gun. Maybe that person who was meant for you will never enter your life because of the harmful, self-destructive decisions they made, whether from drugs or something else. Again, all of this is unfair; there is no way to spin it. However, it is necessary to trust two things: that you will find the greatest path to the greatest happiness anyway (marriage is not a requirement for this) and that you will be surrounded by great people who will still give your life great meaning because of their love for you, and your love for them.

The most important thing to rest upon in this scenario is that it is not your fault—if you are doing everything to the best of your ability. That is absolutely nothing to be ashamed about. Even if you recognize instances where you seriously messed everything up, restoration and fulfillment remains possible. You can still hold your head up because of the potential for your longings to be realized!

When you rest in the reality, with your heart, that some things are simply not your fault, things can radically improve. That realization was the biggest for my personal growth, development, and perspective. Without any melodrama intended, it seemed that the first four and a half years of my seven years of seminary was nothing but extreme struggle and extreme rejection. Seminary was turning into the latest of examples where it seemed to me that "No good deed was being left unpunished." Although I felt my efforts were at their maximum at all times, I also felt that everything was working against me becoming a priest. There were many examples but the greatest and most frequent surrounded the reality that I never really felt part of the community. I would not say I was bullied, but I would certainly say I was not welcomed by most. The single worst turn was about halfway into the seven year program. At that stage of formation, you have your first of two handwritten evaluations from all of the other seminarians. To put it mildly, I was nailed to the wall. Many of them said I should not become a priest and most of their reasons were untrue yet unprovable.

The only reason I did not get immediately expelled was because my record was officially clean. However, I was, more or less, placed on two years' probation with a long list of things that *must* happen at various points during that timeframe, including a stellar review from my supervisor for the internship year which was about to begin. At the very end of the two years I would be evaluated again by all of the seminarians, and this time I would have to receive wholesale endorsement. I certainly do not fault the seminary for this response; they need to be sure, now more than ever, that the wrong individuals are not ordained to ministry. Nevertheless, to say I was devastated was an understatement.

While my immediate reaction was to somehow find a way to work even harder, over the following internship year nothing seemed to work out! If anything the criticisms intensified, especially in the weekly feedback meetings during my internship year. The more I tried the more I seemed to be doing everything wrong. Honestly

I was beginning to feel foolish for even considering the priesthood; that I had just wasted the last several years of my life, along with all of the other sacrifices I had to make.

After a most demoralizing and exhausting Christmas season, all seminarians were called back to the seminary for the annual spiritual retreat. It was there I approached God in my absolute hopelessness. I told God in prayer, "I know I have nothing left to give. I know things have never been worse or seemed more hopeless…" It was at this rock-bottom moment this inexplicable peace came over me. I continued my prayer already transformed by that peace: "But I am going to rest in the reality that I *did* give my all. I *did* give everything I had and everything I am. I held nothing back. I never will. If you want me to be a priest, I will become a priest. If not, you will still take care of me. Either way, I promise I will forever strive to do my best."

I returned to my internship immediately after the retreat expecting everything to stay the same for the second half of that year. I also expected to be told to leave the formation program at the conclusion of that year and somehow I would have to determine how to start all over again. Nevertheless, the difference was that I returned with this joyful peace the likes of which I had never experienced before. I did not work any less. I did not smile any less. I did not give any less. Yet somehow everything radically, instantly, and permanently changed. The first half the year my only sentiment was, "You can do no right!" The second half of the year the only feedback became, "You can do no wrong!" I was constantly being affirmed, even praised, for everything I did. At the conclusion of the year I was given the assessment that I was the best seminarian this supervisor had known throughout the three decades of his ministry. When I returned to seminary at the conclusion of my two years' probation, I was given glowing endorsements from all of my classmates, and I was allowed to be ordained! I now know the success was not so much what I was doing or not doing, but that I peacefully rested in the reality that I was giving my all and truly leaving the rest to God. Nothing else changed interiorly, but everything else improved exteriorly. This little bit of wisdom went a very long way!

Like with all good endeavors, the hardest step always seems to always be the very first one, but the more you can push yourself to face your fears and concerns and uncertainties and express them in the right way, the more you will realize this is one of the very best things you can do for yourself! It is like dieting. The beginning seems hard and unrewarding, yet as more people compliment your weight loss the endeavors to diet further become thrilling for the anticipation of making, and being recognized for, more progress! So in time, you will likely even wish you *always* had these attitudes and behaviors towards your beloved!

A good relationship is like a good building: first you clear the land (Part I), then you place the foundation (Part II), and then you build (Part III). Most relationships die before they have a chance to live simply because a structure is placed upon unfounded land. I recognize this book is heavy with experiences drawn from my life. While I believe experience can be the most effective teacher of all, I hope that the insights, drawn from both my observations and experiences in life and ministry, will ease the process of properly creating and fortifying that truly strong, life-giving relationship! (NB:

All Scripture verses are translations taken from the New American Bible.)

Part I

You deserve the best (How to prepare)

Chapter 1: What true relationships are *not*

"Why do you notice the splinter in your brother's eye, but do not perceive the wooden beam in your own eye?"

—Matthew 7:3

This chapter is fundamental for helping you to realize the relationships you have been longing for. It will help you because it can awaken an awareness of what could have been hindering, or even preventing, the relationships from happening in the first place. I am convinced that the main reason relationships end, or never have a real chance to begin, is because one or both people in the relationship have something in the way. It may not seem to be in the scale of a large wooden beam jutting out of your eye. That is exactly my point. It may seem that the objects which are obstructing your vision are comparatively tiny, negligible splinters. In other words, you may be fully aware of various things about yourself that are less than ideal. Yet throughout your life you may have been dismissive towards these habits, behaviors, misunderstandings, deeply inflicted wounds on our psyche caused by others. You may think they are not a big deal compared with the foibles of others. They may *seem* like negligible splinters but they are truly wooden beams because they have been previously unseen, downplayed or ignored altogether. I hope you will be able to recognize this reality and take steps to remove those splinters more enthusiastically than ever before!

Put another way, I truly believe each of us is our own worst enemy. In one way or another I believe we can often be the main one who sabotages our chances for finding the one God meant us to be with all along. We unintentionally get in our own way of our dreams. We unintentionally trip over ourselves. This takes various forms to various degrees; some are more obvious than others. Based on so much I have encountered in life and ministry, one of the biggest elephants in the room, an elephant that is very hard to ignore, is the backward notion that many people have regarding sex in our society. This is a result of many cultural shifts over the last half century. Many people over the course of a lifetime have dozens of partners in order to pursue stimulation, affirmation, acceptance, bragging rights, and many other reasons which places themselves and their feelings first and foremost. But love is not self-gratification. In other words, relationships are not about answering the question "What is in it for me?" More than ever, I feel this stems from the growing notion that this present moment is all that there is and that you are only as good as your last thrill. I recognize this has happened in various moments of history in various societies, but now also seems to be one of those times when there is a heightened emphasis of the falsehood that all that matters is you feeling as good and high as possible for as long as you can get away with it. I have hoped that this notion would have been largely dismissed by now, as you can look through both the Bible and the history books to see examples where such an attitude certainly did not help those with that mentality!

However, I would simply ask you to examine how dangerous a self-centered attitude is. You may have heard of the Seven Deadly Sins—pride, envy, wrath, gluttony, lust, sloth, and greed. No matter how you look at this list, a false pride is the patriarch of all the others. Every other sin relates to an attempt to fortify our hubris.

Temptations to succumb to self-centered attitudes can be hard to resist while there are so many intensifying pressures from so many directions to conform to this mentality. If you are not actively prioritizing the satisfaction of yourself by using others with little to no thought of the future, you can feel, in one way or another, judged, ridiculed, mocked, rejected, and ostracized until you give into the pressure to run with all the other lemmings over the cliff! *True* lifelong romance is rarely given a chance when the objective is just to have a thrilling weekend, which is why I believe true romances seem more and more infrequent in our world. I did not want to believe it when one of my graduate school professors coolly said, "Romance is the price men pay for sex, and sex is the price women pay for romance." Although I was horrified the first time I heard this, I now believe this sadly is the norm. However, the professor elaborated that "normal" does not necessarily mean "good;" it simply means "common." In one way or another, hedonism is a form of caving in to the insecurity we can all struggle with; insecurities which seem to be triggered in so many easy ways, resulting in-part in feeling an obligation to do things a certain way in order to mask or anesthetize our insecurities. Very often the person I was counseling shared that these experiences have left them not satisfied but objectified, used, discarded, confused, and lonelier than ever before. They hardly felt their own identity, their unique combination of gifts, traits, and talents which make them truly unrepeatable in all time.

Part of our identity is our gender. Men and women are meant to feel their complimentary masculine and feminine identities at all times. It is not a bad thing that women are better than men at some things just as it is not bad that men are better than women at other things. Not just in relationships, but virtually every other area of life I recognize there is the potential for the "whole to be greater than the sum of the parts" where men and women incorporate what is best about them to bring about the best we can all be on an individual and collective basis.

Unfortunately the dilution of gender identity is just one of the reasons I am also convinced that for most, whether they admit it or not, sex is, at best, little more than a very empty experience. Centuries ago Saint Augustine, from his own first-hand experiences prior to his conversion into one of the greatest Christian scholars, likened a backwards approach to sex to drinking sea water. He observed that it only makes you thirstier and thirstier as you drink more and more sea water while getting closer towards death. Science has substantiated that by noting the brain, when a stimulus is not received in the right way, order or amount, is conditioned to demand greater and greater forms of stimulation to feel the same level of the initial high.

I believe virtually everyone can easily rattle off dozens of additional negative impacts of our oversexualized culture that have impacted so many areas of life. I now want to refocus on the reality that approaching sex in any disordered way has negative consequences on *all* of our relationships. We are primarily fooling and hurting ourselves when we give into the lie that anything sexually disordered is not a big deal when the exact opposite is true. One way I can show this is through what many call the butterfly effect theory. Every choice, good or bad, somehow has either a positive or a negative effect on the rest of reality, however seemingly small or indirect. Every positive act somehow benefits all. Every negative act harms all. This has been echoed in many faith traditions, including Christianity.

Conversely, our society claims that, "free love" is love, but it is neither love nor is it free. "Free love" is selfish and harmful. Conversely, real sex is selfless and builds-up the participants. Sex is meant to be an expression of giving oneself entirely to one person without thoughts of oneself. That may sound impossible to some. But I believe achieving this in its purest form can take a lifetime. The sooner we recognize that improvement is a lifetime process instead of a series of mile markers to zoom by as quickly as possible, the better. After all, relationships are always meant to develop and deepen. Sex is one way, within one type, of relationship which points to my belief that relationships ultimately, and perpetually, deepen through our connections with God in Heaven.

Yet I believe that we cannot wait until Heaven; we have to begin striving to live our awareness of the connections of the butterfly effect *today*. Like most lessons, I had to learn the lesson of butterfly effect the hard way. My old attitude was that "I am 'good' 99% of the time so it is ok to be less-than-good 1% of the time." This attitude was a terribly dangerous form of entitlement when we think we deserve something extra, and that we are only going to experience this if we "at least now and then take care of ourselves first and foremost." It was painful when I truly realized the opposite of the butterfly effect is false: that no one can successfully compartmentalize their lives. Realizing the error of this attitude did not occur in one profound instance but after connecting the dots and reflecting upon the habitual damage of my 1%

of bad decisions inflicted against the quality of the 99% of my good decisions, as well as 100% of my relationships.

An example was an experience during college. The first half of the day I was working at a very-important and labor-intensive annual fundraiser. I was invited to a festival later that afternoon to meet up with some friends, but I decided to first treat myself to a few minutes online. This was when the Internet was relatively new, very slow, but just as hypnotic. A few minutes became a few hours, and by the time I made it to the festival, I found out I missed an unexpected opportunity to reconnect with a very dear friend who was also there the entire day but left minutes before I finally arrived!

The butterfly effect can be applied to all relationships, including the romantic ones. There are couples who are already great in so many ways, but they can become so much greater, so much more fulfilled, so much happier if they jettison this one lie: "Being good, dedicated, and selfless 99% of the time towards the other is good enough." More specifically, with the 100% attitude, sex can be among the most sacred, beautiful, and fulfilling of life experiences. A "99%" attitude can jeopardize this. Examples of the 99% attitude that have been presented to me on numerous occasions over the years, include: "If we are not, 'intimate' by the second, or maybe, the third date I break things off," "I have to first test the plumbing beforehand in case we are not compatible," "This is 'Mister (or Miss) Right Now,' not 'Mister (or Miss) Right,'" or "I have needs." We are all meant for much more, deeper, greater, happier, richer experiences than even sexual intimacy offers. It can be part of the path for many, but sex is not a need for all. Needs are on the level of food, water, oxygen … and always striving to give 100% effort towards living the purpose-filled life you were always meant to live—such that all of our relationships, somehow, become stronger.

Everything we have and everything we are is a gift. However, all gifts are meant to be used towards a purpose. I believe that at every moment every person has a very specific purpose, and they deserve every opportunity possible to fulfill that purpose. When we do what we are meant to do, we are fulfilling our purpose at each moment, which is the key to a happy life no matter what that may look like. If we choose not to fulfill that purpose at any given moment, we are hurting ourselves and others for that moment through the butterfly effect. Most of the time when we are not doing what we are not meant to do the damage is not as initially noticeable but it is every bit as real and destructive. One example that I would label as a prevalent one is pornography. Like any vice, people come up with so many excuses to use it, but every time it is causing damage. Little is more contrary to the words, "I love you" than this. I can fill a very lengthy book on the various forms of consequences, both directly and indirectly. It is been pushed as something that would spice-up relationships but they ultimately destroy relationships. One of the many forms of destruction is the pain, inadequacy, and frustrations which result from trying to measure-up to the impossibly airbrushed fantasies portrayed. One or both are left feeling betrayed and humiliated in being replaced with this far inferior, deceptive, and objectified fantasy. What is even worse is that it prevents the living of all of our relationships to the fullest. It prevents us from living-up to the fullest potential and happiness that relationships are meant to offer.

It contributes to a feeling of isolation. Hell has many descriptions, but the worst, and I would argue the most accurate, is that it is a place of total isolation. Nothing feels worse than isolation, and we isolate ourselves whenever we do something contrary to our purpose.

This relates to the other dangerous attitude: "At least I am not doing 'x.'" No matter how, "little, insignificant, or harmless" something may seem, a wrong choice is still a wrong choice—damage will still occur. Life is hard enough without inflicting unnecessary harm upon ourselves, so why would we want to make things more complicated or difficult in any seemingly small way? The end cannot always justify the means. Much more severely, we cannot, as I did much of my life, base happiness on externals. Here is a more subtle, but I would argue equally dangerous, external: the perceptions, the expectations, the demands, and the opinions, *of others*. For so much of my adult life I was miserable trying to satisfy the expectations of others, and I ended up satisfying no one. Happiness within any type of substantial relationship requires that you are at peace with yourself, with the person you were created to be. Besides, comparatively speaking, if you are doing what you are meant to do, if you are doing what you were created to do, then no one else's opinion really matters anyway.

The #1 life lesson I learned, again, like most lessons, the hard way, is to "follow your gut." Virtually everyone continues to struggle with this to varying degrees over the course of life, but you must not spin or misinterpret what your gut is saying. If your gut says "Do not do it," then please do not do whatever your instincts are warning you against. Each and every time I went against my gut, I absolutely made things worse for myself and others. If your gut says, "Do it," then please do it. Even if something did not turn out as expected or hoped, I still got closer to my ultimate happiness, and I believe you will too!

To elaborate, what is the main tool to develop the proper sensitivity to your instincts, and thus enhance a more-constant awareness of the butterfly effect, so that you can consistently improve your ability to minimize those splinters in your eye which prevent the best relationships possible? That tool is imagination! It is one of the most beautiful, and yet one of the most underutilized, gifts from God to help us navigate through everything in life! Prior to making any kind of decision of any kind of meaning, we are able, and meant to discern, with our imaginations, what the likely outcome would be. Important questions to ask include, "What would likely occur if I choose option A? What would likely occur if I choose option B? What are likely reactions from others? What are the likely consequences?" However, the most important question to ask in this, hopefully, habitual, imaginative exercise is, "How will I likely feel?" If you feel unsettled about an option, that option is likely the wrong decision. If you feel this intangible peace, that option is likely the right decision. Without exaggeration, whenever I had truly incorporated this approach I always enjoyed a 100% success rate. This tool is often most handy in the spur of the moment, when something tempts you to do something you know would have severely negative consequences. I always recognized this was a major reason for the success. More importantly, you will be getting closer and closer to your ultimate purpose and fulfillment in life!

Chapter 2: Do not settle

"Life is a banquet, and most poor suckers are starving to death!"

— Angela Lansbury (*Mame*)

As mentioned in the title of this first part of the book, you deserve the best. This is not a shallow, warm, and fuzzy placebo that is pulled out from under you at the first unpleasant circumstance. Each of us, simply by virtue of being the beloved child of God, deserves the very best we can have. This does not mean life does not have its painful, difficult, or unfair parts. It is simply based on the notion that there are good blessings out there that are simply meant to be accepted. We have the freedom on whether or not we are going to accept them. Sometimes I did not see the blessings that were available for the taking. More often than not I did not feel that I deserved them. More precisely I did not feel that I "earned them" or was "worthy of them." However, our true and honest blessings cannot be earned: they can only be accepted. It is also true that we continue to make mistakes and wrong decisions, despite of our best intentions. I deprived myself a lot of happiness throughout my life because I did not think I deserved my blessings yet. This is a form of pride which primarily hurts ourselves but also hurts those we are meant to relate to. If I had accepted my blessings at the time they were first offered, in spite of feelings of whether I deserved them or not, those blessings would have instantly helped me to become a better person. This is because I would be using those blessings to contribute towards new blessings for myself and others.

Another factor in helping us feel more deserving is striving to replace a bad habit with a good one.

I can best illustrate this through the most pivotal moment from my entire life—a few years after I graduated college. Up until this moment I remained in one of the worst vicious cycles I could ever imagine. I was terrified to take any chances in my fear of rejection, so I would not go risk the rejection for the sake of something greater. I would often build up the courage, only to chicken out at the end. After the precious opportunity for a great experience came and went because of my ultimate inaction, I experienced this deep regret and sharp pain. The pain would reinforce my fear of rejection such that when there were new opportunities to experience a fuller richer life, the cycle began all over again. I felt stuck in this miserable feeling that because of this bad habit of this bad cycle, my life, and everyone else, was passing me by.

So how did I break free from this?

During college I developed a crush towards someone whose home was nearby but attended college over 300 miles to the north. The crush was so deep I was paralyzed to ask her out more than I had ever been with anyone. Three years after meeting her I not only felt I finally built-up enough courage to express how I felt, but there was also an opportunity to do so. Nevertheless, in the last moment I concocted some excuses and I chickened out once again. However, I felt this was not just the latest example but the worst occasion of my chickening-out, after I left for the night I experienced this sharpest of sufferings from the regret, far worse, without any exaggeration, than any physical or emotional pain I had ever experienced before or since. I had no doubt it was all because of this my most pathetic experience of inaction. However, from that pain I resolved never to make the same mistake for the rest of my life. I resolved to replace the bad habit of paralyzing fear with the much better habit of taking the chance in a leap of faith. I finally concluded that the pain of rejection could not possibly exceed the pain of inaction!

A year later I would be given one more chance. This time she was in town to help her family move. When we had a chance to be alone I felt my resolve being attacked by the same old fears. I was on the precipice of making the same fatal mistake again when, in that instant, I remembered the pain. I remembered how overwhelming it was. I remembered the promise made to myself. I knew that if I were to choke again the pain would somehow be even worse than before. That gave me all I needed. The fears vanished. I, for the first time ever, finally said what I always wanted to say!

What happened next? She politely said she was flattered but that she was likely going to stay with an old boyfriend. Yet that rejection really did not matter at all! I drove home happier than I had ever felt in my entire life because I not only triumphed over my fears but, more importantly, I realized I was finally free from a cycle that I previously thought would enslave me! I felt all sorts of doors were opened for the very first time ever!

Since that point I have *never once for a single moment* looked back in regret. Of course, I have made mistakes galore and have experienced rejections galore, but I always gave every opportunity everything I got. From this newfound freedom from my old fear of rejection I was able to experience many new activities, meet many great people, and create many priceless memories. Every decision led me towards making the next big decision. The decision I made with my college crush led me to take more chances in every area of life, all of which ultimately led me to taking the greatest leap of faith thus far and enter the seminary in preparations for the priesthood. The rewards ultimately outweighed both the risks and the rejections that occurred along the way. This positive cycle permanently replaced my old miserable cycle, and I am most grateful to know that this positive cycle never has to come to an end. Yet, most importantly, this has helped me ultimately develop this growing peace of knowing I would always give everything my all!

From this lesson I concluded that some of the worst things that happened to me were also the very best things that happened to me. It can be the same for you. Please remember there are only two types of suffering: redemptive, or wasted. Suffering is often unavoidable, but when it is handled with a spirit of trust and openness on how to better move forward with the pain caused from the suffering, that suffering will never be a total loss.

What leads to the loss of relationships is that some people settle for less than what they were meant to have. It is not because they feel they do not deserve it, it is because they gave up on finding the very best. I feel now my eyes are more open to this reality. By late childhood I began to formulate these ideals mostly related to that type of person I wanted to have a relationship with. Each quality I deemed nonnegotiable. Each quality was a must, a minimum trait I knew the ideal person had to have in order for there to be even a chance for a true relationship.

One trait of all relationships, romantic or otherwise,

is that they are meant to give and renew life, not just for the person you engage with, but for yourself. With all of the challenges, difficulties and pains of life, we need that renewing, peaceful breath of fresh air that is most especially found in true relationships. Saint Paul observed with both our human bodies and the body of a religious community: *"If [one] part suffers, all the parts suffer with it; if one part is honored, all the parts share its joy"* (1 Cor 12:26). But just as connected as the parts of the body are, so also is our body is connected to our soul. We are meant to have relationships that are so beneficial for the soul. This can be experienced when you feel a weight instantly removed from your shoulders merely by seeing the person! I have enjoyed that feeling numerous times. It is among the best feelings I have ever experienced, and I also believe it is the type of feeling we need to encounter now and then in order to help us insure we are carrying our burdens from life in the best way possible.

Some ideals, fortunately and thankfully, get refined as we mature. Some are just plain childish, and hopefully everyone realizes that on their own before it is too late and the consequences are irreversible. I began to give up on believing the traits I was searching for in a person even existed. Part of the reason for this was that I was given the impression that my ideals were unrealistic.

Even worse, I unfortunately, like most, was pressured to think my ideals were insane. Because I succumbed to the pressure, I not only began to give-up on the existence of my ideals but I made the bigger mistake of settling for far less than the best, oscillating between the notions that this lower standard was as good as it would get or, that this lower standard was at least better than nothing or being perpetually alone. Consequently, more and more I replaced my ideals with what I thought other people thought were the ideals, such as having an official social media "status." I was compromising away from what I was meant to have, simply checking off something in the to-do list of life. Please avoid these pressures because I do not know of any instance, my life included, where this ever ended well.

One consequence was that checking off steps became my prime motivator. Of course I wanted to give my heart to that special person, but I was also driven by this motivation to get to certain milestones by certain stages of life. At best I reduced dating to this accounting-like mechanical process of scrupulously completing an order of steps. At the very least I ended up constantly, and unnecessarily, beating myself up when I fell short of this impossible process. This exasperation took off the day of college graduation. Several pairs of classmates were engaged the same day! I was thinking it was likely too late for anything for me but isolating singlehood! This was exasperated by social media, as the pages displayed my friends appearing happily married with seemingly perfect kids! But it is so important to realize that not everyone is meant to get engaged at 22! In many cases it is better to get married later. Yet, because I did not yet recognize that I made more poor choices. They unnecessarily complicated my life and the lives of others at best and prevented me from reaching my fulfilment soon at worst. I came close to passing the point of no return in some of my mistakes. I came close to being stuck in living a façade of a life where things seem happy, but they were not. I can only offer my mistakes in hopes that you do not make the same wrong choices which can only make things more complicated and difficult.

The worst consequence of going down a slippery slope of repeatedly making the wrong decisions is becoming someone that you are not meant to be. This is not to say anything bad about anyone. The truth is quite the opposite. When you are the person you are meant to be you are the very best you can be. You are precisely your best being the person you were created to be at each moment. The people who will like you the right way for the right reasons will recognize that. The timeframe may not be to your liking, but what ultimately matters is that things turn out the way they were meant to, even if that takes longer for you than it does for others. Once it happens, you will not mind so much that it took longer than you originally hoped. You will just be happy that you did not compromise and you patiently waited and persevered.

Hopefully you eventually realize that relationships are much more than one big happy date. Through relationships, together, you are meant to face, and work through, all of the challenges of life. But in time you can realize that this is better than your original understanding, because relationships are more than surface-level highs. They are opportunities for communion and understanding the likes of which you never thought possible with anyone!

Compatibility should be one of those nonnegotiable factors. More specifically, romantic compatibility can be ascertained based on how naturally you get along in most other areas of the relationship. Once you know you have found the right one with whom you wish to marry, I believe that you can rest assured that the compatibility will continue to grow and develop after the wedding vows are exchanged. This is a reason why I promote abstaining from sexual intimacy until the marriage occurs. In this case, you will not be depriving yourselves of the absolute greatest meaning that can be found within a sexual encounter for those who are called to that form of intimacy, an intimacy which I believe is best suited within the radical lifelong commitment of marriage.

The best things in life never seem to come easy. Yet no one is meant to give up too soon. No one is meant to forfeit the potential to find greater freedom, peace, and happiness. Our core true desires are not unrealistic but a very central part of the person we are meant to be. Our deepest, truest yearnings include feeling important and not feeling alone. These yearnings go hand-in-hand. We do not feel alone if we feel important to someone. There are those who will always find us most important to them! There are those who will *not* find your most important ideals foolish. Please do not give up on your non-negotiable ideals in looking for that special relationship! Please do not settle for anything less than the person who was meant to help you live your life to the fullest, the way you, and only you, were meant to live!

Chapter 3: Recognizing self-worth

"The man recognized and found again his own humanity with the help of the woman."

— Pope Saint John Paul II (*On the Dignity and Vocation of Women on the Occasion of the Marian Year*)

This is now a good point to share some of the best advice I have ever received: "Take your time!" While we need to do all we can as soon as we can, we need to do everything in the best way possible. By taking our time our process of healing will not be in the form of a flimsy bandage which easily goes away, but a fortified cast which makes us stronger than we had ever been. So please be patient with yourself as you continue to persevere in removing the splinters which kept you from wholeheartedly seeking and obtaining the relationship you are longing to have. It is likely an ongoing, lifetime process of refinement and polishing. But the more you are able to remove some of the splinters which blind our vision, the more you can see your self-worth. The closer you will be able to see yourself as you truly are.

I also thank you for your patience with me up to this point in the book. At the very least, by recognizing more of the obstacles to true relationships and by simply seeing more clearly what relationships *are not*, you are far more prepared to enter into true relationships than people who never stop to think about how these factors could be impeding their happiness.

For many, people think that all there is to relationships are parts that actually have nothing to do with relationships. Maybe your previous notions of relationships have even left you feeling doomed to isolation. But as I alluded to earlier, we are never meant to do anything in isolation. We are never meant to do anything alone. This is different from solitude. We all need times where we can be alone with our thoughts and alone with God, as Psalm 139 beautifully reminds us: *"Where can I go from your spirit? From your presence, where can I flee? If I ascend to the heavens, you are there; if I lie down in Sheol, there you are. If I take the wings of dawn and dwell beyond the sea, even there your hand guides me, your right hand holds me fast."*

We most especially need the help of God. However, just as people are placed in our lives so we can help them as God's instrument, others are placed in our lives so that *we* can be helped *by them* as God's instrument. For most, this is how an exclusive relationship is ideally structured: each person simultaneously and mutually helps the other become the person they were always meant to be. This is one way where the couple can feel like they are truly one person; what is most important to one is most important to the other. This was beautifully displayed to me many times before, including by a couple married several decades. They both explained that because they feel that part of their very self is always with the other, they can never feel alone, even when they have to be physically apart.

I once believed the false notion others have of independence. Independence, in the form of being able to provide for oneself when you are able, can be a source of good pride. However, early on I was mistakenly convinced that independence meant instead doing everything all alone, without anyone's assistance whatsoever.

At times I was even left feeling that seeking assistance from others was an occasion for feeling inadequacy, failure, weakness, and even worse feelings.

I am confident many share this sentiment because our culture seems obsessed with perception. It is ok to convey as much as possible the perception that you are a person of integrity, honesty and authenticity. It is not ok to craft the perceptions we give based on seeking the standards of approval from others. I believe that is both impossible and is a wasteful endeavor.

I believe we all want to make a positive contribution to our world. I believe each of us is meant to make a difference no one else in time was ever meant to fulfill. The longings to do so are among my very earliest memories of any kind, so I would even argue it is my very earliest longing. However, it is not a sign of weakness to acknowledge that we need help from others in virtually everything we choose to undertake. It is essential so that we realize that we need to receive, but in the right ways and at the right times. In one way or another I feel this is the keystone of the entire book: Being able to recognize the *need* to accept love. Yes I believe that we are meant to give without holding back, but I also believe that we are meant to receive without holding back! This was beautifully illustrated by Jesus himself: "*Give and gifts will be given to you; a good measure, packed together, shaken down, and overflowing, will be poured into your lap.*" (Luk 6:38). No one recognized the need to receive love more than Jesus did. The gospels frequently depict Jesus trying to go off to pray to God the Father. Again and again he receives the love, renewal, strength, motivation, and, especially the serenity, to be able to give what he was meant to give each day. Just as we are meant to give love and nourishment, we need to receive love and nourishment from others in different ways, times and amounts.

I say this to emphasize love is that it is not a score-card. If your significant other loves and gives more or less than you that is not an occasion for the other to be concerned about being behind or needing to catch up. True love does not keep track of such things. It does not care about who has more or less points. In true love one only wants to love the other as much as possible. In the right match, the other simply feels, and strives the same way. The sooner we can accept that reality the better, because accepting this will remove the notion that we are able love best or the most on our own.

One of the greatest, and most necessary, benefits of our ability to accept love is that the power of that love can contribute to healing the wounds of our past which haunt us in so many ways. Everyone has brokenness that needs healing. Everyone can improve in one way or another. Everyone has new opportunities to love at every moment. None of this can fully happen without accepting the love you need to receive without shame. We are never meant to feel shame. Certainly at times we are meant to feel regret and repentance. But we are never meant to feel shame. We are not meant to feel shame because, regardless of what we do or don't do, we have a dignity through our humanity.

I certainly recognize that dismissing all the feelings of shame is much easier said than done. I recognize that it is not as easy as flipping a light switch. I can certainly relate to this reality. I also know from firsthand experience that if left unchecked shame only poses the danger of making everything worse. Regardless of whether it was imposed upon you from someone else or it came as a consequence for your own decisions, it feels shame has a way of sinking its claws deep into our being. I feel nothing can contribute to isolation, at its worst, than shame. The degrees of shame may be different, but the more we allow shame to convince us that there is no one out there who would not condemn us the more we begin to dislike ourselves, and the less we feel like we can accept the love of God.

Overcoming shame involves directly countering the lies it claims. First, there are people out there that we need to, and must, reach out to for help. If you are meant for marriage your partner, both before and after marriage, must be someone upon which you can count. Maybe it is also a minister, or another true friend, or a psychologist, or a physiatrist, or an anonymous support group, or a combination of these. But the most important one to approach for help is God. If God created everything and worked all the miracles of time, why should we doubt that we can untie the knots which led to our shame? Although God knows us better than we know ourselves, he longs for us to talk to Him, to express everything to him, including our longings, our wounds, our sins, our fears, and our doubts! Because you did so you will be able to better receive all the love that God longs to give. Does this sound too good to be true? Saint Thomas is my proof. He was likely deeply wounded and filled with shame for abandoning Jesus in his darkest hour of his crucifixion. The shame led to a refusal to believe without feeling the marks on Jesus. But Jesus, instead of blasting Thomas for his doubt or telling him that he blew his chances for salvation for acting the way he did, loved him and granted his request, simply saying *"bring your hand and put it into my side, and do not be unbelieving, but believe*" (John 20:27). So, if Thomas turned out ok, why should we still doubt?

In all of this, however, please be patient with yourself as you persevere through the process of becoming freed, once and for all, of shame. It may take years, but I believe that once you are truly free from shame, you are free from it forever, if only because you realize that it was nothing but an unnecessary misery.

Yet freeing yourself from shame also involves the efforts of truly loving yourself. Although we are never meant to feel shame I believe with all my heart we are meant to have a profound humility. The best definition of true humility I have ever found is that it is seeing yourself exactly as you are, no more, *but also no less*: seeing yourself as the beloved child of God, as if you are the only child God! This is echoed from the beginning of the Bible: "*God created mankind in his image; in the image of God he created them; male and female he created them. ... God looked at everything he had made, and found it very good*" (Gen 1:27, 31). We are from God, we are beloved by God, and we need his help, particularly his guidance. One compass used by God to lead us on the path of that true humility is the other, particularly if you are meant to dedicate your life to someone else in marriage. They acknowledge that some things you get right. They also acknowledge that you can be better with other things.

I also feel compelled to present another, connected Bible verse: what is considered the great Commandment of Christianity: "*You shall love the Lord, your God ... you shall love your neighbor as yourself*" (Mat 22: 37-39). From my own life and from my daily experiences in ministry I feel that in its truest sense the third part of this great Commandment is the most neglected; to love God and neighbor "*as* yourself." I will never encounter a word as neglected as that "as!" Right there with loving God and neighbor, we are commanded to love ourselves. I hope you realize that true love does not equal self-indulgence. It means that that the more we can accept that we are loved by God as we are, and the more we can accept the potential to be loved by our neighbors as our brothers and sisters under God, the more we cannot help but love ourselves. It is not optional, we must love ourselves if we are to live the life we are meant to live and love God and our neighbor in the right way.

A major way we must love ourselves is by forgiving ourselves. There are so many ways we paralyze ourselves, but one of the worst ways is an inability to forgive oneself. I see much of the unnecessary tortures I caused myself when I refused to forgive myself. I missed out on so many great experiences with great people because I was afraid of causing more harm. I cannot emphasize enough the need for self-forgiveness as quickly and completely as possible. However it is often not as simple as only saying, "I forgive myself." Like with all things, we need to ask for God's help to truly forgive ourselves and not to relapse into self-loathing when memories of the related event recur. The recurrence will happen but it is our opportunity to remind ourselves that we have already forgiven ourselves and that we are resolved not to make similar wrong choices again.

The more that profound self-love is recognized with your heart the more everything radically changes for the better. It is precisely through this love that we simply become who we were always meant to be. Through that love our outlook improves such that less and less can threaten either our peace or the plans to do what we are always meant to do. Yes, we are meant to love others, and it is tragic when someone does not receive the love they are meant to receive. But we simply need to receive. No mental gymnastics are required. No advance planning of how to pay it forward or backward. Simply renounce the shame, swallow the pride, and enjoy. It is so essential that you find the other who is able to, as much as possible within their own limitations, give the God-like unconditional love we all need in order for you to become the person you were always meant to be.

Regardless of the other particular traits you may have on your list of requirements for the person to marry, this one trait should be on everyone's list: the ability to have a relationship with someone who is able to love you the way you are meant to be loved. You need to be loved as yourself. You need to be loved *for* yourself. You need to be the person you were always meant to be. The biggest con of all is this lie that we have to be someone other than we were meant to be. I have had so many people lament to me about how phony the profiles look on the online dating sites. Although the profiles present the person as the best catch ever, I just as often hear how the person they met looks very little like the person presented in words, accomplishments, and photos. They seem at best, gross exaggerations. This is because the person often presents themselves as something they are not. They embellish their better traits and imply they have no flaws whatsoever. This is because they feel that they have to portray someone they are not in order to be accepted. This creates a ticking time bomb, and, sooner or later, potential relationships disintegrate.

Another reason why I believe true love is ordained by God is because people are loved, in spite of, and sometimes even because of, their self-perceived flaws. Regarding the right person, you will not shock them. You will not disappoint them. They will, in fact, *delight* in you at every moment simply because they love who you are no matter what comes to the surface—and one way or another everything needs to come to light.

Part II

What is needed to start the right relationship (How to start)

Chapter 4: Overcoming fears and weaknesses within your control

"So do not fear or be dismayed."

> — Deuteronomy 31:8 (364 other times in the Bible)

The last sentence of chapter three may have filled you with fears galore. There are many things you may have long before concluded that nobody could *ever* see! You may have also provided yourself with proofs that such a secretive approach was justified, especially with those who were closest to you. Maybe you have even felt that the slightest revelation of the slightest flaw would leave you feeling exposed as a fraud. After all, that is akin to how Adam and Eve sadly felt when they first realized they were naked. But this is just one reminder of why we are *directly* told in the Bible 365 times, once for each day of the year, to not fear.

The moments to be resistant of fear will always be the opportunities to become better with each moment of life, because you are not allowing anything within your control to hold you down. President Franklin Roosevelt was absolutely right during his timeless speech during some of the darkest days of the Great Depression. In a very real sense the only thing we really have to fear is fear itself, as fear by itself can be very destructive. You are not capable of having the best relationships possible unless you are always *striving* to overcome your fears in order to be the very best person you can be.

Nothing can paralyze us more than fear. Nothing can take us away from our true purpose in each moment than the fear of countless external variables throughout life which are ultimately, and often completely, beyond our control. In a particular way, there are circumstances when things painfully did not work out in spite of our best efforts. However we cannot allow that or anything else to foster, or fortify any fears. Nothing can become a license to fear the externals beyond our control. We also love to feel like we are in control, but the externals which are beyond our control can still hurt us. We cannot recklessly disregard the real dangers which may threaten us. We are meant to take reasonable steps to mitigate our risk, but worrying about anything does absolutely nothing to improve things. At best, worrying keeps us from making the most of the present moment. At worst, worrying becomes the wrench thrown in to prevent the realization of our ultimate plans, relationships, and purpose in life by blinding us to miss out on seeing some of the greatest blessings of our entire lives, blessings that were often right in front of us. In seminary we were given the fable of two friends who walked outside their classroom for a minute of a beautiful autumn morning. One saw, and marveled at, the glorious beauty of the rainbow of foliage on the trees and on the ground. The other missed seeing such beauty altogether because he was too worried about having enough time to rake all those leaves! Others have shown me that when you incorporate a fear-free approach nothing can bring you down, such that even the worst of experiences can bring you closer to God. An extremely profound example was when I was asked to meet with someone recently diagnosed with cancer. Although I expected to meet someone overwhelmed with anxiety and uncertainty, this person was overwhelmed with gratitude for the precious gift of life. They expressed their conviction that every day is meant to be enthusiastically embraced! That made all of their challenges much easier to face!

The question I feel we need to habitually ask ourselves is: Why do we want to make life unnecessarily more difficult by fearing and worrying over what is beyond our control?

I am sure that while you can offer your own litany of fears there are many parallels from even just this tiny part of my litany: Fear of people thinking the wrong thing about me. Fear of people being disappointed in me. Fear of embarrassment. Fear of failure. Fear of rejection. Fear of not having enough. Fear of the unfair. Fear of being labeled a loser. Fear that we are ultimately going to be the primary culprit of messing everything up. Fear of ultimately destroying everything in our lives. Fear of not having a purpose. Fear of letting go of grudges for harm caused. Fear that I am truly alone. Fear of not being understood. Fear that I will ultimately scare away anyone in my life. Fear that my way is the wrong way. Fear that I have to do it all alone. Fear that the pains of the past will keep haunting me, regardless of whether caused by myself or others. Fear that I will never be free of wounds that continue to cloud my judgment. Fear of exhaustion.

I was certainly exhausting myself in all these fears! This was because I did not yet recognize the meaninglessness of fear.

I can pick apart every fear listed, and, you can with the help of others. We must, logically expose the lie of the fear as part of the process of freeing yourself from fear. We can pick apart the first one from my litany: people thinking the wrong thing about me. So many people are so unhappy because they have been motived, consciously or not, by notions on what others think, how to gain everyone's affirmation. It is very sad when people let others' opinions overrule their own convictions of the direction they need to take in life. Some are not shy in sharing their opinions yet they neither lift a finger to help, pay attention to the flaws and insecurities in their own lives, nor are they even thinking very much at all about that person while they are not with them. So why is their approval worth not doing what you were meant to do?

It is not enough to renounce your litany of fears. They must be replaced with a litany of loves. Love we are called to share. Love that remains constant, even when it seems to go unappreciated. Love that will bring ultimate peace and fulfillment. Love that is uncomplicated. Love that is confident. Love that is to inspire and console others as it radiates the reality that we are loved by God. Love that is instantly responsive to the present need. Love that is total, unconditional, and inexhaustible. Love that we can spend eternity contemplating. Love that is being offered in spite of our flaws. As I have echoed regarding other processes, please recognize that this is unlikely to be instant or cold turkey but will occur gradually over time. To draw an example from our litanies, if you fear embarrassment seek opportunities to foster more opportunities to display your confidence in being a person who lovingly adds value, maybe through getting involved with service organizations or formal social groups. As long as you are striving to let go of the fears and replace those fears with opportunities to love, the growth will continue, even when it feels that little or no progress is being made.

Yes, those gestures of love can be sacrificially difficult, but those often turn out to be among the greatest experiences of all!

I would also argue that the best way to progress is with the right person accompanying you. They can become your greatest shield against fear. Through them we are empowered to conquer our fears once and for all! At the beginning of a relationship I feel everything important needs to be communicated as clearly as possible: your expectations, your hopes, your promises, your fears, your weaknesses. I look back and laugh at the reality that in the past I attempted so many relationships without communicating anything of substance, never mind these fear factors. More specifically, people fear to reveal their weaknesses because they do not think the right person will give them a chance, such that they will instantly and totally be rejected. The exact opposite is the truth: the right person is meant to help you overcome your weaknesses! They will delight in you revealing them in a respectful, clear, and trusting way. They will be honored, thrilled, and zealously motivated to show their love of you precisely by taking the opportunity to help you overcome them! They will lovingly help you overcome whatever hurdles, whatever scars, whatever weaknesses you have been afraid to reveal to anyone, even to acknowledge honestly to yourself. You can find yourself, in time, finding a transformation of attitude regarding your fears. Instead of wanting to hide anything which holds us down, we will happily and eagerly sharing our deepest, and perhaps darkest parts of ourselves, knowing that, far more than merely receiving the benefit of the doubt, you will continue to be unconditionally loved so that you can properly bring everything to light for all to be seen for what it truly is, allowing us to become better prepared to love unconditionally more and more frequently!

The right person will truly long to help us become the best *version of ourselves*! To clarify, we need to immediately jettison the notion that any of us are meant to be the best. We are not meant to be the best. We are, however, meant to be the best we can be. There always seems to be someone better than us at particular things anyway. You see that in the sports world; records eventually get broken and re-broken over and over again.

When we are the best we can be we can find ourselves overwhelmed with an additional motivation to overcome all of our fears, along with the conviction that we will overcome them once and for all. To do this I find it helpful to name all of the fears out loud so that we can see the worst fears for what they truly are: illogical, empty, meaningless, and in-charge over us for way too long! Please keep saying out loud, "By the power given me by God I renounce you ____! I am not going to fear you ____!" God has given you the ability to do this, and we are meant to do so with conviction, and as many times as you feel you need to say it out loud.

It is one of the greatest, most liberating, and most peaceful experiences when you recognize that someone is not only accepting you for who you are, not only helping you break-free of all fears, but also making you feel like the most important person in the world even while you still have the flaws you are attempting to shake.

Chapter 5: Friendship

"The capacity of living the fact that the other—the woman for the man and the man for the woman—is, by means of the body, someone willed by the Creator for his or her own sake. The person is unique and unrepeatable, someone chosen by eternal Love. The affirmation of the person is nothing but acceptance of the gift, which, by means of reciprocity, creates the communion of persons."

> — Pope Saint John Paul II (*The Man-Person Becomes a Gift in the Freedom of Love.*)

At the final class period concluding six semester credit hours of graduate courses on Church law, the vast majority of which was spent pouring over the intricacies of what is required for a valid marriage in the Catholic Church, the professor asked my classmates and I, "Since I hope you know all by now what is required, who could tell me what is *not* required to have a valid marriage?" The answer was shocking: "Love."   Although this may be true in terms of Church law, I cannot imagine a couple approaching the challenges and opportunities of marriage without love. Those who say, "I married my *best* friend" have a factor I consider most important for the truest demonstration of love within happy marriages: friendship.

There are many levels of friends, and social media has done an outstanding job diluting this reality further. You click a button to accept a "friend request," and this someone, who may only be a robot, is now labeled your friend on your social media page. The spectrum of what is often captured within the word friend is diverse, and includes acquaintances, buddies, associates, hang out friends, fair-weather friends, and many others.

I am absolutely not decrying these degrees of relationships. Quite the opposite is true, as it often could be nice and important to have people in different areas of your life for different reasons including recreation, renewal, life-enhancement and many other benefits. Most people meet their spouse through one of the sub-categories of friend. However, I am cautioning you not to place more value upon these types of friendships than you should. I am not saying anything bad about anyone. Yet making a relationship larger than it is can lead to painful disappointments that often leave the person feeling more isolated and hurt than before, more reluctant to even try to open-up to the hope of having a best friend. I am confident you have had most of these experiences with those you previously considered friends: Maybe you felt that you were taken for granted, that the friend only interacted with you when they needed something from you for a time. Maybe you were abandoned when the things you previously had in-common with the friend (school, work, club, shared-location) no longer existed. Maybe the friend simply got tired of you and wanted to move on to someone they think is more interesting. Maybe the person who you thought was your friend hurt you from doing things they thought were no big deal.

I caution you because I want to spare you from the consequences I experienced when I over-valued relationships. I was so hurt that, for a time, I resolved to keep everyone at arm's length, keep the walls up. I simply resigned myself to the reality that the notion of friendship

I was looking for simply did not exist. It reached a low point when someone approached me out of his genuine concern for me to tell me, "You do not say very much about yourself." But the worst part was that I thought he was paying me a compliment about my armor shielding me from getting hurt again!

This is all precisely why I need to focus on the concept of *best* friend. The older you get, the more you realize that very few people are meant to journey with you throughout the majority of your life. Most people who are in your life are meant to be in your life, but only for a time, just like you are meant to be in many people's lives but only for a certain period of their lives. For most people in our lives, we may care deeply for them and they may care deeply for us. Yet we may only need to see each other for a certain period of time and for a certain frequency. Again, none of this is saying anything bad about anybody. None of this is ultimately bad. This is actually a great reality because it emphasizes the extraordinary value of just one special person, can have one you throughout most of your lifetime! For the best friend, there is never enough time or never enough frequency. The best friend will also feel the same about you! The main reason for this is, as Ecclesiasticus 6:14 notes, *"Faithful friends are a sturdy shelter; whoever finds one finds a treasure."*

The keystone of the treasure is this: a true friend will always, and genuinely, simply want to be with *you*—just as you are! They rejoice when you rejoice they are sad when you are sad. You will always feel the same about them. Recognizing this allowed the necessary healing from all that prevented you from enjoying your blessings to the fullest.

Because the time with a best friend can be the best use of one's time, you actually miss the other more with a higher intensity between each encounter. You begin to miss them while you are still with them. It is in part because of the nature of true friendship—the peace, communion, enjoyment, and gentle challenges to be your best. But most especially you feel that you are with a part of your very self, and that you are delightfully resting in the reality that they are resting in a part of themselves through you. This kind of friendship can never plateau. It only grows deeper, happier, more fulfilling, and peaceful, all through the inevitable challenges of life. This is the kind of friendship that heals from the past, taking you from wanting to be a loner to wanting to do everything with the other. This unique category of friend, which is often hardest to obtain, can truly be called a soulmate.

When I use the word soulmate, I mean this person feels like a very part of your very self. Because they feel the same about you the mere thought of being apart from them for extended periods of time is intimidating at best. I believe that finding each other's soulmate is a must for marriage.

Chapter 6: Natural reciprocity, a.k.a. quantum entanglement

> *"Furthermore, the communion of persons could be formed only on the basis of a 'double solitude' of man and of woman, ...* All that constituted the foundation of the solitude of each of them was indispensable for this reciprocity. Self-knowledge and self-determination, that is, subjectivity and con-sciousness of the meaning of one›s own body, was also indispensable."
>
> — Pope Saint John Paul II
> (*General Audience, November 14, 1979*)

I always felt that I was trying to run away from my-self, that I was trying to be someone I was not, thinking that the real me would only repulse others. I think we have all at one time or another experienced pain from the look of repulsion from someone. Please rest assured that is more, if not completely, because of something that person still needs to work through. If you recall nothing else from this book, please recall this: you are meant to be loved exactly, *and even because of* the person you are.

After you believe you may have found the one you are meant to share life with in marriage, waste no time sharing all the things which are most important to you. Please also encourage them to do the same. Too often people ironically withhold those tidbits until it is too late for the relationship. While a large degree of compatibil-ity is very important, this does not mean you will always like all the same things in the exact same way. It certainly does not mean that improvement is not needed. There will always be opportunities to do things better and we will always need help with that.

What it does mean is that because you chose to reveal yourself you will be truly and genuinely loved *and liked* by someone else! I believe we all long to be liked as much as we long to be loved. I believe we need both. Sometimes love feels too universal, akin to the mentality that "everybody gets a trophy!" Being liked seems more specific, akin to the reality that "I am drawn to the unrepeatable combination of traits that makes you who you are!"

Something that seems far more valuable than ever before is the gift of time. We may amass great amounts of monetary wealth, but we are only going to have so much time to spend. So when someone chooses to spend their limited time with you and you chose to spend your time with them it is a most beautiful precious exchange. That is simply because you are at peace with yourself through the other. You are with the best part of yourself. You have this true, and total, communion where everything feels right. Everything feels at peace. Everything feels comfortable. Everything feels safe. You feel most like yourself. Your resolve is stronger against any threat to this safety and security.

It is what you have in common which creates the bond. It is a sign that you are meant to be with that person, and a sign that you will not experience loneliness again. This is why you cannot say "I love you" too many times. We are meant to say it with our heart each time, and to that special someone we are meant to say these words as many times as we possibly can, and in many specific *ways* as you possibly can. More likely than not, rather than tiring of these true expressions of love, the other will only delight in them more and more. While saying, "I love you" is so important, showing that love is equally important. One way we show it is by looking for every opportunity to treat our partner. To surprise and delight them as much as possible in ways which will not only lift-up their days, but also make them realize how much they are cherished, and how you are treated simply by their existence.

Remember that list of traits I made for the ideal person? Even though I inevitably gave up on that list, it was an important reflection of what I thought I needed for a relationship to work. At the very least these traits reflect the longings which can motivate us in so many ways. We genuinely want to strive for the traits that you not only deem important, but also necessary for that right relationship! Now when I am speaking of ideal traits I am not speaking of such comparatively shallow things such as measurements and hair color. I am referring to activities and interests which you would both share, to unique personality traits, and how they handle the various highs and lows of life. Most importantly, I am speaking about ideals that, in one way or another; we should all be striving for: selflessness, compassion, honesty, candor, good values, understanding, and the like. These are the traits that are truer, and can last infinitely longer, than the physical ones. All of these surround the longing we have for someone we can rest in securely. Conversely, I can trace every last one of my failings to an insecurity that I am not going to be as loved and esteemed and delighted in as much as we want to love, esteem, and delight in the other. This will result in a restlessness which poses many dangers. It can keep us from simply enjoying and resting in the moments and blessings we do have with that special someone. It can create insecurities which can create a fear which can drive us into doing things that not only compromise the enjoyment of the blessings but will also threaten to harm ourselves and those around us.

Again, trust is a must for true love. Trust is a must to enjoy the blessings we are meant to enjoy even as we are surrounded by so many threats and dangers and pains which will remain largely outside of our control.

In this case you can trust that the person with all of the important traits you are looking for exists, and that you have all the traits they have been looking for as well. This can be an indication that you were indeed truly made for each other! However, not even this by itself can be enough. I made that mistake to a degree when I entered into a relationship with someone who looked good on paper. It looked like we would at least have compatibility at a surface level. There needs to be something more, something deeper. It comes under so many names: the spark, the zing, the click, the moment, etc. But it is another must. It must also be mutual. It must also, at least in-part, be something indescribable, something intangible. In seminary I was told the fable of a wife who asked her husband of several decades why he loved her. The husband proudly gave a litany of all the many great traits she had, the things she did extremely well, and concluded by saying, "and this is *exactly* why I love you!" This left the wife heartbroken because she knew she did not feel loved for the greatest, most important quality of all, the intangible one.

I cannot emphasize enough how important this is. The other qualities and actions are nice and important, but there must be this trait which words fall short to describe. It must be this trait that you know will always be there, just like a heartbeat. If there is no heartbeat, there is no person. If there is no indescribable trait then there is no special relationship. At least for this life, the other traits may all cease to exist; the other will not only change physically as they age but they may also no longer be able to take care of the most basic human activities. You witness true love when you witness the other still happily doing everything, and I mean *everything*, for their beloved.

What does this trait look like? It is a trait which leaves you feeling with something even better than happiness, as wonderful as that is. The trait leaves you with a peace which allows you to persevere through whatever challenge may lie ahead of the both you over the rest of your lives together; a peace that fills you with the desire to do absolutely nothing else but to express your love for them.

Part III

What is needed to make the relationship soar (How to keep)

Chapter 7: Pure appreciation of true beauty of the other

"It is Heaven all the way to Heaven"

— Saint Catherine of Sienna
(*original source unknown*)

Most people think of how to obtain a relationship. Yet few seem to think ahead about how to keep a relationship. Just as behaviors are developed over time to both prepare and to find that one true relationship, there are behaviors that likewise need to develop over a lifetime in order to preserve the relationships. The key behind these habits is remembering that relationships are meant to grow better, stronger, and closer. If they are not constantly improving they are somehow disintegrating. But rather than looking at this as a challenge or chore that never ends, our perspective needs to be that this is a precious opportunity to find new and better ways to show our appreciation of the gift we have found in our partner. Yet, as if that was not motivation enough, over time it will likely get easier in a sense to constantly grow and enhance your relationships, as you build momentum from realizing the fruits of these new behaviors. Like I said before, please be patient with your development. Your beloved will be patient with you!

It always amazes me when someone pushes back at a church when they learn they have to have a preparation period of at least several months before they get married. They feel ready to get married as soon as they can book the caterer and the honeymoon. They seem to forget that the better the endeavor, the more preparation is necessary. It takes several years of intense preparation to become a doctor, priest, lawyer, or military officer. So, it is understandable that many marriages fail because there was virtually no preparation. I believe this failure developed over generations, and it is largely the fault of many. The more we become aware of our dependency on God, the more we recognize our need to be guided by Him, through the teachings, teachers, and leaders of our faith, on how to best approach everything.

The greater the endeavor, the more we need the help of not only leaders but also of our families, our community and the Divine. It is for this later reason that I believe everyone should be clamoring for the wedding ceremony to occur in their houses of worship. It is hard enough to take care of ourselves. Being responsible for another and for the creation and upbringing of even more individuals through a family requires all of the help we can get!

Ideally, marriage preparation does not begin, but is nearly finalized, with the engagement ring. It is ideally the final stage of determining once and for all if you are prepared to commit the rest of your life to this one other person. In a sense marriage preparation begins shortly after birth. Within one's family there is meant to be a daily demonstration of what the partnership covenant of marriage and family life looks like within the various situations of life. Marriage is intended to be displayed in the context of one's larger church community, where they are shown how such relationships are also both a part of a larger community as well as a necessary grace from God. They should also demonstrate transparency and reliance upon divine assistance through prayer. It is actually a sign of strength and wisdom to recognize that we cannot handle things on our own. Pray for that strength from God. Pray with your loved ones for everything you need, as we are reminded by Jesus, *"where two or three are gathered together in my name, there am I in the midst of them"* (Mat 18:20).

Sadly, many lack this necessary foundation when preparing for marriage. Through no fault of their own they were often deprived of that love that was meant to come from their parents. However, it is still possible to learn as much as you can so that the relationship can flourish as much as it can. We cannot choose the family we were born into but we can certainly choose the family we are meant to create. We all long for that true family, but biological relation is never a requirement. And that, in one form or another, is grounded upon true love. Every couple is meant to prepare to make their vows. There needs to be as thorough an understanding as possible of what this means before they are given.

"I, ___, take you, ___, for my lawful wife/husband, to have and to hold from this day forward, for better, for worse, for richer, for poorer, in sickness and health, until death do us part."

It is obviously easier to focus on the upbeat parts of one's vows, but what about "For worse? For poorer? In sickness?" If everything was always happy, peaceful, and easy there would be no need for anyone to even make any vows whatsoever. There would be no temptation to quit. The purpose of the vows is precisely to help us through the hard times. They are meant to be our anchor of support to weather the difficult times. If marriage is your vocation, you are meant to lean upon the vows, just as you are meant to lean upon God, and just as you are meant to lean upon your beloved.

Although some occasions are easier than others, those called to marriage are meant to constantly strengthen their marriage through the vows. One, perhaps unexpected, example is by always respecting boundaries. Every person has boundaries, even spouses with each other. The kneejerk reaction may think that boundaries would be a bad thing in marriage: "We are one flesh now, why would there be boundaries?" Instead of seeing boundaries and restrictions or limitations, they are a means to insure that we are respecting, delighting in, and loving the other to the fullest and best way possible in which you can discern for each and every moment. What a beautiful way to say "I delight in giving my gestures of love to you far more than I delight in anything else!" What a beautiful way to thank God for the gift we received in the other, akin to the way Adam first joyfully exclaimed upon gazing upon Eve for the first time: *"This one, at last, is bone of my bones and flesh of my flesh"* (Gen 2:23)!

This bible verse segues to the *way* of respecting the boundaries of the other: treating that person as a literal part of your very self. After all, this is the reality in the marital bond. You want to be treated as a respected, unique, and valued person, so why would you now want that even more for the person you love more than any other on earth? This is your compass. Because you always will be directed towards your concern over what is best for the other, you will be best able to love the other in the best way moment to moment. This is much more than giving some physical space when you are told they have a headache! This includes seeking out ways to uplift, help, and affirm the other as the treasure that they are! In any given day there are truly dozens, if not hundreds, of opportunities to do so. *This* is respecting boundaries! This is the path to the deeper delight that comes from reverencing the person such that you are making sure you are always placing yourself *after* the object of your affection. You are appreciating the beloved in the best way possible at every moment.

The opportunities of the path of growing in peace and happiness together through the mutual respect of boundaries is a major reason why I loathe the phrase often used to describe marriage as settling down. To me it implies that the best days of your life are forever behind you, that excitement and happiness are over, and now the best you can hope for is this boring and numbing routine and drudgery. It also more tragically implies that love sooner or later cools like an ember. Who in their right mind would ever want that? But for those called to the vocation of marriage, the excitement should just be *beginning* on your wedding day! I have told every couple I have assisted in wedding preparations that, while I hope their wedding day is perfectly happy and enjoyable, I more particularly hope and pray that it will be far outweighed by many happier days in their future life together! This is because, as one, there will be more great opportunities to grow deeper in love and truly life-giving experiences than if you had never married!

Regardless of vocation, every action in every moment is *always* the real opportunity to show your love. It can be more fun to express that love while actually doing something fun such as a vacation, but it is far more profound to express that love during the routine, the stressful, and the overwhelmingly painful and difficult moments. Express that love without a trace of the tone of "Look at how much I love you." Sounds like a fairy tale, but I have seen it numerous times, and it is truly the most beautiful thing I will ever see. This is why it is so extremely important to do everything you can to get rid of everything that can keep you from loving the way you are meant to love.

Something that has helped me, and many others remove the seemingly insurmountable mountains in our paths to happiness was having a small, tangible reminders of who you love. Maybe it is a small photo, a song from your playlist, a small note, your smartphone wallpaper, or some other small personal memento of the beloved which you can carry around with you everywhere you go! Looking at, hearing, or clinging to this item may be, and often is, reminder enough for you that with God's help and the motivation to love you can overcome almost anything! Most particularly, it reminds you the love you have for the other is infinitely greater and more meaningful than whatever obstacle is seemingly threatening you at that moment. That is another demonstration of how every moment is that opportunity not only to show just how capable you are to love, and how much you treasure their love.

Every activity, every moment is the opportunity to ask, "Is this the best way I can love, or is this counterproductive?" The more often you choose the better way to love, the better and more frequent opportunities you will have to show an even greater love, and the more easily you will find yourself purely, freely, happily, and enthusiastically embracing those opportunities to love. This is partially because more and more you will also recognize what is contrary to your opportunities, what is wasteful and worthlessly threatening your appreciation of those most important blessings you have right in front of you, blessings which may disappear if they are not recognized and appreciated.

The key to this appreciation is gentleness. It has been described as a very fruit from God. You naturally become gentle when you realize that the gifts you have, particularly in the other, are meant to be treasured. When we make the wrong decisions we are acting in a spirit contrary to gentleness.

Chapter 8: Allowing the relationship to thoroughly enhance life

> *"Iron is sharpened by iron; one person sharpens another."*

> — Proverbs 27:17

This is my favorite Proverb because it summarizes the best way to be purified while casting away one of the greatest lies of all: that we do not need each other. To varying degrees this is this main purpose of every relationship and every encounter. We strive to make the other person better while the other simultaneously makes us better. We not only automatically become better, more purified if you will, each time we place the other first, but also in doing so we allow the other to purify us! Out of their love for you they will want to make you as happy as can be, and that involves you becoming the best person you can be. Meanwhile you will keep feeling more strongly motivated to do the same towards them. That mutual desire will only cyclically grow and deepen as you realize what the other is doing to help you. This can easily become the best form of motivation to become your best.

I feel most people take the opposite approach, even in relationships, and they become hypercritical. Often to make themselves feel better about themselves, they simply pounce on anything and everything that is not seemly perfect with the tone of "There is something wrong with you; you need to change."   This approach often results in the receiver feeling discouraged with a rotten taste in their mouth. Instead, when someone genuinely kindly, lovingly believes in you, encourages you, cheers you on, focuses on how the already-present positives can be improved, it is very hard to resist that motivation to accept their words of invitation to become even better!

Relationships, particularly in marriage, are not 50/50 they are 100/100. Many have this notion that "If each of us do 50% of the work, we can do the minimum but still meet in the middle in completing what we have to complete." But that is never how life works. Sometimes you will need to be the stronger person. Sometimes your partner will. The frequency and duration will always fluctuate. What matters is that you are always giving your all presuming that the other is doing the same, thoroughly in every area of life.

Most people shortchange themselves because they feel they can set aside little boxes for themselves, thinking "It is ok to coast and veg out for this while." We best show our love and appreciation and value for the other when we are doing exactly what we need to be doing at every moment. Sometimes those moments include rest and recreation, but they are always for the sake of that appreciation through always being the very best we can be at every moment. Every decision we make. Every action we do. Every interaction we have. Every word we say. Yes, even every thought we have.

Why should there be no exceptions? Exceptions are a way of saying, "I love you only 99.9% of the time." Do not get me wrong, we will still make mistakes, we will still have misjudgments, we will still inadvertently hurt, but the important aspect is that we will be always striving, always trying to be our best, and that is precisely why we have literally nothing to fear. I fear one of the deepest fears we have is that our best efforts will result in failure. That is why people hold something back however small. They tell themselves: "If this blows up in my face at least this sliver I held on to will remain unharmed and in my possession." But it is more often than not that sliver that can mean the difference between success and failure.

This is a great spot to elaborate on what I mean by the importance of always respecting boundaries. As difficult or awkward as this may feel in the moment, one of these best things we can often do is to always emphasize the perpetual openness of the lines of communication. Even here the notion of being one flesh fits perfectly. You can recall times when things got worse because you did not even communicate with yourself, when you said to yourself "I don't want to think about that aspect of myself of my life." Just as we need to be honest with ourselves we need to frequently, and verbally, encourage are partner to not keep it bottled up. If someone has a flaw of being overly argumentative, their partner can overlook that part of them in recognizing their true value, but they should still be able to sit down and talk about how that flaw can create more, and unnecessary, problems both personally and when dealing with others. They should specify how they feel that such flaws are not respectful of their boundaries. Everyone should be open to improvement, especially when knowing the change positively benefits all. You want your beloved to benefit because you love them. You want to be better because you love your beloved.

The key is to always remember, even when it is not expressed, we are still loved and appreciated by the other. They cannot help it, and they know they are loved and appreciated by you! This makes all the noticeably happier moments even happier! This is yet another motivation to always strive to be and do your very best, even when your beloved is not around. This is the very essence of integrity: being your best even and especially when no one seems to be watching. At the very least, there should be a gradual improvement of less and less time- and life- wasting activities and towards more and more fruitful activities. These moments are not only intended for activity but for rest. The professor of my class for Holy Orders acknowledged the need for ministers to have times of rest. Rest is not for their benefit but for the sake of the people receiving the ministry. To summarize, everything you do should also answer the question: "Is this the best way I can love in this moment, both directly and indirectly?"

The other reason why I emphasize the importance of never discounting a single moment or activity is because everything in life is connected. Because everything in life is connected everything can be the once-in-a-life-time opportunity to determine if we are living and loving our best way. Even in the most seemingly insignificant activities can reveal the most significant opportunities to remove forever those things that deceived us and caused us so much pervasive harm—the things which prevented true trust.

Chapter 9: *Surrender:* Ongoing transparency, honesty, and trust

"Love cannot exist where there is no trust."

— Edith Hamilton (*Mythology*)

But being your best does not occur in insolation or in a vacuum. It occurs only with the help of others, especially that one special person. "Only" is not a word to be used loosely. But, why settle for 99% when you can have 100%? Everyone is meant to have 100% of what is available to them. So the *only* way true relationships work at their 100% best is if you reveal everything, and I mean *everything*! In revealing your deepest darkest parts of yourself, trust that the other will not only still love you but will become more *in* love with you because of your trust. They will also be delighted to help you be healed from everything once and for all! Most relationships fail because weaknesses are not addressed or even acknowledged and they often become time bombs sooner or later. Yes, saying and hearing these things can be excruciating. I shudder at all the times I fooled myself thinking that, "If I do not say anything, my problems or weaknesses do not exist." I made life so unnecessarily painful with that attitude, particularly in my relationships. Yet I was fooling myself more than I was fooling anyone else!

Pain is the opportunity to show how much we love. Never count the cost, but delight in the other in each and every single moment, even the bad ones! I remember my shirt from high school track and field conveyed this grain of truth by stating, "Pain is weakness leaving the body."

This is awareness accompanied by enthusiasm that you will indeed be free of the major source of your unhappiness through the tender perfect help of the right person. Just as you are meant to see the other as they truly are, the other is meant to naturally see you for who you are truly are. When everything is seen in its proper perspective, you are already a great person as you were created by God. Any and all flaws, large and dangerous as they may be, are cumulatively, comparatively speaking, a thin veil that needs to be removed so the real you can be seen! Unfortunately people often hear about the opposite: that the person they fell in love with and the person they married are two different, opposite people because there was never true total trust.

To elaborate, a major reason why dating can be as stressful is that the persons will not only put on what they may think is the best face but at every moment will also mask, even deny, the existence of traits they feel will be a deal breaker in the relationship. This is another time bomb waiting to happen if everything is not revealed in the right way and the right time. Otherwise thing may explode out of you in the worst way at the worst time, like a neglected pressure cooker, and the other is devastated with the perception that you have somehow changed for the worse. It is so important to realize that when the beloved loves you, they love the entire person that you are, in spite of the parts you wish would immediately disappear. This true unconditional love is the most powerful weapon to vanquish those traits that you never wished you had.

That is why absolute honest *transparency* is another must. After all, God knows our value. He knows every part of us, even the parts we wish He could not see. But

He still loves us and longs for us to accept His love in all of its forms. We accept that love directly through him and indirectly through others. We show that we accept this love by striving to love unconditionally and trusting that we will not lose God's unconditional love on account of our transparency. It may be painful before you reach that point however, just like it is painful to truly acknowledge our faults and flows to God and to ourselves. If they seem to run for the hills the moment you reveal something deemed by them to be less than perfect, then that is a pretty good sign you are not meant to be with that person. For the sake of both people, both of you need to discern if you are meant to share a radical transparency with each other. It can be scary, but if you are both committed to that transparency it will be as mutually beautiful as what is revealed on your wedding night!

The opportunities for transparency extend to all situations and circumstances. Those are opportunities to immediately squash the fear that wells up the various unexpected and stressful triggering moments of life which can be so easily upsetting. In the heat of the moment we do not always recognize the connection between the trigger and our old hidden wounds. The wounds trigger fears. The fears trigger the temptation to keep the wounds hidden. We do not always have the luxury of stopping in the frenzied busyness of life to talk things through. Yet as soon as we properly can, we need to bring everything up. If something is bothering you, tell them. If you have a fear, express it. If you have an ongoing struggle, let the other know your gratitude for their help you in that journey to freedom. A most valuable lesson I gained in my counseling courses is that as emotion goes up, the ability to think goes down. In any tense moment, please remember that how you say something can be even more important than what you say.

A whole other level of this transparency is the simultaneous transparency the other will be giving towards you! Trust can be the most sacred and beautiful gift that can be exchanged. There should be a joyful excitement to knowing that the other is revealing far more about themselves to you than to anyone else. Knowing that the other person trusts you will make you strive to be better. The best part is that by allowing the other to help you heal, and by being healed, you also turn out stronger than you ever thought possible, freer than you ever thought possible, and happier than you thought possible. Your beloved has the potential to enjoy the same, all because of you!

This is why transparency can be the most beautiful form of surrender.

Yes, this surrender is required in order to be freed from the major scars and wounds and fears we feared we would never be released from. But surrender is also required in order to appropriately handle the arguments, debates and discussions that arise from daily life. This message is echoed throughout this book: life is hard, but there are so many ways we can spare ourselves so much unnecessary strain and suffering. The first step is not keeping anything bottled-up inside. You need to let it out in the right ways and circumstances, but you need to let it out! We can all recall examples where we know we made things far worse than they already were by not letting things out. Again, your beloved will long to know if something is bothering you. They will want to do everything they can to free you from your pain. But surrender also certainly continues in the acknowledgement that you are not always right all the time. We are gifted our brains so we can strive to use them in the best way possible. My childhood pastor said what is most lacking in the world was common sense, that ability to think through and project what the consequences would likely be for one decision or another, all based upon the hard facts you already know. Even if it turns out to be the mistaken, albeit well-intentioned, decision, the lessons learned from it can contribute towards you making a better decision. In surrendering to the love of God and to the love of the other, we can determine the best direction to take for the one you love.

This is why, no matter what the give-and-take looks like, no matter how humbled or exhausted you may feel at the end, things must end on the element of enthusiasm: the belief, from your heart, that things will somehow, in the realest sense, be the best way they can be from this moment forward. You can see how things could have been done better in the past, but that is your springboard into your resolve to doing things better in the future. That is a critical part of keeping your eyes on the big picture of what really matters most!

Chapter 10: Courage through perspective of the big picture

"It is indispensable in order that man may be able to 'give himself,' that he may become a gift, that he will be able to 'fully discover his true self' in 'a sincere giving of himself.'" — Pope Saint John Paul II (*General Audience, January 16, 1980*)

Courage simply means doing what you know you are meant to do each moment ... even when you do not feel like it! Courage is the difference between "good" relationships and "great" relationships. I hope everything

I wrote so far makes one realize that you need to have the courage to reveal your deepest darkest parts to the other in order for them to help you heal. I wish I could say this courage is a one and done sort of action. But like so many things in life, it requires you to persevere through the challenge of saying yes to that courage over and over, sometimes from one difficult moment to another. It is all about trusting that you must choose the courageous decision knowing that it is precisely your path to freedom from what has made you so unhappy for way too long.

Before I realized this, one of my truest friends observed all of this by how I was going about everything in a stressful, frenzied manner. He concluded that I had to go much easier on myself, which is why he felt compelled to offer a most profound bit of unsolicited advice from which I believe most people could still benefit today. He simply said, *"Don't be a hero!"*

"Don't be a hero?! How can this be? I always thought heroism was something deeply admired by all and something to aspire to always!" It took me a very long time for me to truly understand what he meant. I found at least two profound meanings in this phrase of wisdom containing only four words! This is the first meaning I gleaned: Do not hide behind a misconception of heroism. Do not hide behind the notion that you always have to save the day and then immediately fly off as a lone ranger to single-handedly extinguish the next fire drill, before going to the next, and the next, always doing, fixing, and giving but never ever stopping to breathe. I believe we already have a Savior: God! So why should I burn myself out as a faux-savior when we were all already saved? Besides, we may think we are saving the day by constantly doing, going and giving, but

not one person is made to live this way. We may think we are saving the day by single handedly doing all the time, but if we are, the quality of our work may simply not be as good, and we may actually be making things worse. In a specific way, we may dangerously feel that as long as we are busy saving the day in our super-hero uniform, no one will ever learn of our true secret identity as a flawed individual. Nothing hinders the good we are able, and meant, to do more than ignoring the flaws which get in the way.

This is why the second meaning behind my friend's advice *Don't be a hero* is equally important: true heroism requires teamwork! Simultaneously receiving while giving! This is the ideal, and this is most perfectly demonstrated in my faith through the love given between the Three Persons of the Holy Trinity. The Holy Trinity is a theological concept which has, and will continue to, confounded all of the greatest theologians. One of those theologians, Saint Augustine, asked how it was possible to squeeze the concept of an infinite eternal God into our limited, finite individual brains. There will always be more knowledge to be gained. But for here and now it is simply enough to state my belief that at each moment, and for all eternity, God the Father, God the Son, and God the Holy Spirit are constantly giving everything towards while receiving everything from and through the other persons. We need to always strive to imitate this model of love.

As you overcome your fears with your beloved, you delight to play your part to free your beloved more into their identity. They will only delight in the fact that you are simultaneously helping them as they are delighting in making you the person they know we were always meant to be. They are elated to realize the potential they recognized in you very early on!

Here is another benefit: the more into your identity you become, the more the *true* hero you will be able to become. This can apply to any flaw, but judging falsely is one common example. When you connect wrong judgments damage it has caused in your lives or in the lives of others, you may have had the resolve to stop that habit. But it takes that special person to help you truly see through all that you have to do to get rid of it. This is what did it for me: I had a headache and I took an aspirin. A little later I was asked by a friend if I took something for my headache. I instantly, falsely, judged that the person did not think I knew how to take care of myself. But I quickly learned that this friend did not think this but that they simply wanted to offer me some aspirin! That instantly convicted me to the heart. I recognized I falsely judged that I was being falsely judged by that someone who only, and purely, wanted to love and help me. That gave me the motivation to never give-in to the temptation to falsely judge ever again. The memory of that has since substantially decreased my frequency of falsely judging, which in turn helped me to more efficiently help others in my life and ministry!

Upon reflecting upon this lesson more deeply, I realized that none of us can ever judge anyway. No matter how smart you think you are, it is literally impossible to think of every possible scenario or every possible thought that is going through another person's mind. Life is challenging enough already, so why put ourselves through the added stress and series of mental gymnastics? This is just one example which shows that one person can help you, at the very least in motivation, overcome everything that is keeping you from being your very best.

Saint Francis de Sales constantly reminded his congregation that every moment of every day you are only moving forward or backwards towards your true identity. Every decision, every choice either helps or hinders on this. And you will notice progress all along the way. You will see, however seemingly small the important strides you will be making all of the time because of your courage.

Chapter 11: Forgiveness and sacrifice through gratitude

"He accepts her as she is willed 'for her own sake' by the Creator, as she is constituted in the mystery of the image of God through her femininity. Reciprocally, she accepts him in the same way, as he is willed 'for his own sake' by the Creator, and constituted by him by means of his masculinity."

— Pope Saint John Paul II
(*General Audience, January 16, 1980*)

The more you can love, the less you can think about yourself. This is because you are thinking more about the object of your love and why they are so loveable. When you think about marriage it makes perfect sense that you would want the best for the other, you have both become *one flesh*. You are one person. This is why, when preparing couples for marriage, I inquire further if they plan on having shared bank accounts. Everything you have is meant to belong to your partner, and vice versa. The moment you consummate your marriage, and every time you renew that act of consummation, you are reminding each other that you are literally, continually gifting your entire self to them. In marriage, you become one, so why would any aspect of your life reflect that you are still two separate individuals?

The reality of being one in marriage is why forgiveness is most important in marriage. It is essential to have repentance for the times we know we did wrong, to recognize that it would have been better if we never did those actions, and to wish that there was a way we never made those choices in the first place. While I believe in the impossibility of turning back time, I am even more convinced, many times over, that God allows no sin to go to waste if we truly accept him and his help with our hearts. That help is most powerfully given through forgiveness, which can become the greatest catalyst towards realizing how much you are loved and the greatest motivation to love others more than we ever thought possible. Jesus himself recognized the explosion of the desire to love as a fruit of forgiveness. In response to the woman's acts of seeking forgiveness, Jesus declared, *"So I tell you, her many sins have been forgiven; hence, she has shown great love. But the one to whom little is forgiven, loves little"* (Luk 7:47).

Forgiveness can come about more easily when we can have the true perspective of time. When we are hurt by someone it can feel completely pervasive as if that is all there is. As sharp as the pain can be, the reality is that it is only meant to last for a certain amount of time. Forgiveness is so critical because unlike the pain of being slighted, some relationships are meant to last forever. Saint Therese of Lisieux, who lived in an obscure cloistered monastery with little formal education, is recognized as one of only 36 Doctors by the Catholic Church because she had this insight. She confidently wrote that not even death could separate her from those she loved, and she even wrote in *Story of a Soul* that she "would spend her Heaven doing good [for those still] on earth." These reminders of the eternal potential for some relationships magnifies the importance of doing whatever it takes to, truly, give and accept forgiveness as early as possible.

I would always hope we would never want to cause a situation which will require our forgiveness. Yet even with everyone's best intentions, we all will inevitably need to engage in true forgiveness.

There are two sides to forgiveness: the one who needs to receive the forgiveness, and the one who needs to give the forgiveness. The more genuine each side is, and the more simultaneous the sincerity is, the more powerful the forgiveness can be.

Regarding the one who needs to ask for forgiveness, there is a spectrum of seeking it: On one end it involves the one who harmed saying in a half-hearted manner, "I'm sorry."

This partial contrition may, and often is, sufficient to knock down the first domino towards partaking in a truly transformative forgiveness which enables one to love more than they thought possible. But more often the mere saying that you are saying sorry, without the sensitivity of the damaged caused, is tenuous at best and dangerous at worst. Without an awareness of the damage caused there is an increased risk of repeating the same behaviors.

That is another reason on why a deeper level of contrition is preferred, where the power of forgiveness can cause radical improvement. I believe this radical level is a gift from God. Forgiveness can never be earned, only accepted. The key for accepting in contrition, feeling truly sorry for the wrong we have done which brings about a sharp turn in our direction in life. It is a key element of conversion because we regret of our sins from the core of our being. We regret it so much we are repulsed by it and want to avoid anything that could ever bring even the possibility of committing that action again. We are repulsed by it not only because of the damage it caused us but more so because of the damage it caused to our relationships with others.

I believe that when we realize with our hearts the pain we caused when someone was hurt because of our wrong choices, the pain can be as stinging. This is one of the reasons why forgiveness is such a radical act of love: the one harmed chooses to alleviate the suffering of the other who truly realized they have done wrong. It is when the recipient of the forgiveness realizes this radically large gift of love through the forgiveness, the desire to show gratitude in every conceivable way for that forgiveness can be at least as overwhelming.

It is so important to genuinely and quickly offer forgiveness, even when it is not asked of you. Regarding this type of forgiveness, I have often quoted the words of a friend who has been a prominent Baptist minister of several thousand for decades: "regardless of the hurt you experienced always leave the door cracked open." This was most profoundly expressed by Jesus *while* he was being crucified, words which capture the most radical action of time believed by Christians as the ultimate act of forgiveness of all time: " *'Father, forgive them, they know not what they do* '" (Luk 23:34).

When given the right way, forgiveness is all benefits and no drawbacks. For one, forgiveness stops the bleeding, stops the further damage which can slow, or even prevent, the fruition of God's plans through you.

When we are wronged, the sting can be among the sharpest. The worst sting is this feeling of betrayal when the source is the person we last expected it from, the person we thought would never intentionally hurt us, the person we thought knew us much better to even be tempted to hurt us, particularly when we were complete-ly innocent of anything which would warrant that harm. But, as bad as the harm is, withholding forgiveness caus-es additional damage to oneself by allowing the betrayal to foster a self-poisoning, and often blinding, resentment which can cause far more damage to everyone around you if left unchecked.

However, as alluded to earlier, that does not mean you become a punching bag or doormat. The one be-stowing forgiveness, has a right, and a duty to talk, about what caused the harm in the first place, as the Jesus re-minded us, "'If your brother sins [against you], go and tell him his fault between you and him alone. If he listens to you, you have won over your brother.'" (Mat 18:15)

I think that one of the greatest tragedies is when the lack of forgiveness prevents the truly great relation-ship from developing into marriage, or from surviving, or from even starting! Conversely, when forgiveness is approached the right way there can be a greater anticipa-tory excitement for the future than ever. This enthusiasm becomes part of the resolve which accompanies the for-giveness. Once our eyes, and hearts, are opened to the realization that avoiding such behaviors and habits will improve everything else in life radically, we can hardly wait to begin afresh, especially when it is with the one person we are meant to love more than any other!

As if that was not great enough, forgiveness is just one way of contributing to the never-ending cycle of bursting with motivation to show in actions your our deepening awareness of what a treasure you have found in the love of your life, the person you were always meant to marry. Since I was twelve it has grieved me to think that most people could think of moving on to another person thinking that the *one* is replaceable. "The One" is irreplaceable. This is why finding that one can be our deepest dream. Once we find them our new dream becomes doing all we can to radically show how much we love the one we have found; the one who has found us. You love this person so much, that if they were meant to marry someone else, and did, you would feel happiness for them! I have proposed this radical scenario past several couples married over fifty years, and they unanimously agreed. Fortunately, if you are meant to marry each other you never have to worry about this scenario, but I have seen the same radical love demonstrated in couples in many other beautiful ways in various forms and in various stages of their marriage. People have shared with me that, in spite of the very real pains and difficulties which accompany scenarios such as unemployment, loss of property, infidelity, absolute total incapacity, and many other situations that would not want to be approached otherwise, they have still loved the other.

I would argue that what is most radical is that through all of the ups and downs of life, through all the delightful and painful life-changing moments, is both the giving and accepting of ongoing forgiveness. It can remain the most radical way to love, in every action, every emotion, every thought, every fear—all done in the right way. It can often feel like the greatest of sacrifices because they often are!

The best description I have heard of the verb sacrifice is: to make holy. As shown by Jesus, the greatest way anyone can show love is through sacrifice, and you must know that these opportunities to love in this extreme are not just through forgiveness but in virtually endless other ways: Giving-up your preferences for the sake of your beloved, making substantial, significant, and profound changes in your life both in the long- and short-term, the sacrifices of the most precious resource of time.

There are countless moment-by-moment sacrifices made in the process of raising children to become the people they were meant to be! However, I have often shocked those preparing for marriage when I emphasize the reality that you are meant to always love your spouse first and foremost. Nothing, however noble, can become an excuse to compromise that. However, the best indirect way to love your spouse is through your children, as these children are the result of your collaborative love in so many ways! A child is the single greatest tangible gift we can receive in this life. Even if the child was not ideally conceived from the absolute love between two spouses, the child remains the precious responsibility of those in whose care they are placed! The way they love later on in their lives will be largely based on how they were loved—how they were the recipients of your sacrificial love!

All of this may sound like too much, which is why we must remember that we cannot do it without God's help. With God's help, even in the worst of tragedies we are somehow led to something good. The main purpose for relationships is helping each other get into heaven, so in when that becomes our primary focus, we are all but guaranteed the help of God.

When you find the one you were called to marry, and when you approach that relationship the right way, things will irreversibly grow and deepen. Even in the seemingly routine or mundane moments you will be growing always closer, always freer, always wiser, always happier, always more in love!

The desire to love will be so huge it will feel like it is consuming you! This is because you are also filled with gratitude for this person—and for God who brought this person into your life. This love and gratitude will also bring you closer to God as your eyes open more to not only how much you are loved by God but how much you are able to love in return through a true gratitude!

As children we think gratitude was simply saying "Thank you." But as wisdom is gleaned from the experiences of life, we learn that gratitude is expressed in how you live. Cicero observed thousands of years ago that, "gratitude is not only the greatest of virtues but the parent of all others." Gratitude led me into seminary. It does not matter what you have to do, or what sacrifices you have to make, or what you have to endure. Once you recognize the way of showing the world how grateful you are, you are willing to do anything. That is why I chose to enter seminary to prepare to dedicate the rest of my life in the priesthood. Even the process before the first day was demanding, overwhelming and painful. But as can be inferred with earlier anecdotes, the challenges, pains, sacrifices, and rejections would only continue throughout the several years involved in seminary formation. Yet, no matter what, at each and every painful moment I felt this was the best way to express my thanks. Even when some of my ex-military classmates stated how seminary was worse than boot camp, I always realized the rigors were for the sake of fortifying for the sake of loving God's people in the best way possible over the rest of our lives. I can easily fill the book with many specific examples, but I feel the point is conveyed: I did it all out of gratitude for the indescribable blessings I had received in my life up to that point. That gratitude was always my peace.

I offer this illustration to show that with gratitude you can handle virtually anything. I feel there are few motivators better than gratitude. Gratitude is certainly a sign of your acknowledgment that God is with you helping you every step of the way. Gratitude can be our assurance that we can face any challenge or uncertainty of the future. They are among the greatest opportunities to show just how much you appreciate your gifts—especially the gift of the other. Those opportunities can truly extend to each moment!

Conclusion: The importance of rest and humor

"*Marty, the secret to a happy marriage are three words: 'Let's eat out!'*" — William Bihler (*said on the occasion of his 69th wedding anniversary to his wife Charlotte*)

I wrote this book in my hopes to lend a hand towards the fostering of as many happy peaceful life-long marriages as possible. I realize much of what I wrote made fantasy look more real, but I know it is real. I believe that if you are meant for marriage, if you pursue it as best you can, and if the one you are meant to be with is doing the same, it will happen. What's even better is that by fulfilling your purpose you will be giving others a new-found hope for their lives simply through the example of your marriage.

I understand the reluctance to believe this, because we struggle to count on more than one hand the number of truly happy marriages. But I believe even one happy marriage is proof enough. I want to offer the example of this one married couple of nearly seventy years. It was always clearly obvious to me and everyone else that they were deeply and happily in love with each other over this decades-long partnership. Well into their nineties they seemed to maintain this exhilarating youthfulness while being as sharp, independent, and active as ever, as they participated, and ran, several prominent church and volunteer ministries. What was more amazing is that it was through their radical love for each other that they always seemed to have plenty of love to share towards everyone else!

Their foundation of love began amidst the challenges of World War II. It was continually fortified in their careers, entrepreneurship in a new business, the raising of their four children, relocation to the other side of the country, health scares, heartbreaks from tragic news from their children, and several other trials. Nevertheless, they not only lovingly leaned on each other in their lifelong partnership throughout, they grew more madly in love with each passing year. When I finally had the courage to ask them their secret to a happy marriage, he gave a perfect response which made his wife beautifully nod in agreement: He simply said: *"Let's eat out!"*

"Let's eat out!" For me three short words addressed two musts for any relationship in one simple phrase. He was not so much emphasizing a need to dine out in various restaurants as much as the need to *relax*. Life is packed with unavoidable difficulties and challenges. No matter how rare, limited, or infrequent, we must make time to rest with, and *in*, our relationships. Sometimes that can be, at most, for a few minutes a day. But I can relate that sometimes those few minutes made all the difference. To insure we have the time needed we need to make sure that we are not spending time doing what we are simply not supposed to do.

For me that was only learned after much time and pain. Yet once I accepted it nothing has become more liberating. I used to feel plagued by guilt at the thought of saying no to anyone's request to do something that I was not meant to do. However you look at it, there are only 168 hours in any week, and we simply cannot do every activity that is out there. When I did not say no at the appropriate times, I stretched myself too thin and the quality of everything I worked on suffered. Yet once I realized that saying no was not necessarily an impolite or wrong, I immediately noticed not only an improvement in my health, but also an improvement of the quality of everything I chose to say yes towards, particularly within my relationships.

Equally important to *how* we rest is *why* we rest. For example, all vacations seem to fall into two categories: Restful, or counter-productive. The latter leaves the feeling of being more exhausted after the vacation than before. However, the breaks we can find need to be as restful and balanced as well as fun and enjoyable. Please balance out travel and/or fun activities with good reading, prayer, reflection, and true rest. Most especially, take time to grow those relationships which matter most, particularly with that soulmate! It is so important to remind each other *why* you love each other. As important as it is to return to daily life rejuvenated, it is even more important to renew your perspective of the blessings of all of your relationships so that you may fortify the resolve to prove your appreciation of those blessings in new and deeper ways!

If you struggle with feeling guilty about taking these breaks, remember that no one understood the importance of true rest more than Jesus. Repeatedly he went off to pray and rest in his relationship with God the Father. And he encouraged is disciples to do the same. Even Genesis depicts God resting on the seventh day after completing creation by the end of the sixth day. The best interpretation I have encountered of that part of Genesis is that although God himself certainly did not need to rest, he simply wanted to admire and enjoy the beauty of His creation.

You may ask, "What about marriage?" or, "What about having children?" Certainly there is no day off from either of these! However, that does not remove the importance of finding whatever opportunities you can for true and meaningful rest, even with your family and children.

While the words of my friend's advice, "let's eat out" was a succinct yet powerful way to convey the importance of rest, the way he said it also succinctly conveyed the importance of maintaining your sense of humor!

My childhood pastor, who continues to work in various ways at 90 years of age, believes the world needs to adopt a better sense of humor! We may not be able to do much about the world's sense of humor, but we can certainly do something about our own! I feel this last point in some way connects to everything else written in this book: the need to laugh at yourself. We are not perfect, but we are called to always try to be perfect. Jesus himself simply told us to "*'Strive to enter through the narrow door'*" (Luk 13:24). We are going to make mistakes galore; we are going to fall short, but the opportunities to improve will never end. A hallmark of you becoming a better person is constantly discovering new and different ways to be better. However we cannot take things too seriously.

Laugh about those things about you and your beloved that are not perfect in the eyes of all. Some of these traits, if not harmful, can even be among the traits of the other in which *you* delight the most! I believe, contrary to those who believe in reincarnation, we are only passing by here once. Make the most of it by resting, laughing with, and delighting with the other. Regardless, and even in spite of, all of the other difficult and painful things of life, through resting in each other always you will radiate the reality to all that we are ultimately made for happiness, and this happiness is not a fairy tale! This is simply what one priest knows about marriage!

Author Bio

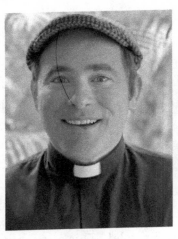

Rev. Martin L. Dunne III is a priest in a very large church community in Boca Raton who previously spent a decade in the, "real world" between university and seminary. Those experiences included completing a Bachelor's Degree in Accounting (& later a Master's Degree in Divinity, which incorporated several graduate-level courses on counseling), obtaining the Certified Public Accountant License, commercial business management, home ownership, leadership in large non-profit organizations and several romantic relationships. These experiences, along with the many profound insights and experiences gained in years of ministering to people and couples from many walks of life, have resulted in a unique perspective on what best helps make relationships succeed.

CPSIA information can be obtained
at www.ICGtesting.com
Printed in the USA
FSHW010329160121
77628FS

9 781649 214843